GHOST STORIES
of
CHESTER COUNTY
and the Brandywine Valley

by Charles J. Adams III

EXETER HOUSE BOOKS
2001

**GHOST STORIES OF CHESTER COUNTY
AND THE BRANDYWINE VALLEY**

For information, contact:
EXETER HOUSE BOOKS
P.O. Box 8134,
Reading, PA 19601

FIRST EDITION 2001

PRINTED IN THE UNITED STATES OF AMERICA

ISBN 1-880683-15-6

TABLE OF CONTENTS

FOREWORD

The spread of universal education, the increase in the number of newspapers and magazines, the movies, and the radio are rapidly causing the loss of all traditional material. It is the more urgent, therefore, that whatever remains in the minds of our old folks from earlier and less strenuous days be recorded before it is lost. This applies especially to such regions as our own Chester County.

The words are those of J. Alden Mason, who in an undated essay, "The Folklore of Chester County," encapsulated many folk traditions and beliefs and urged that those–and stories of ghosts and haunted places–be treated with respect.

Toward that end, Mason also wrote:

The collection and study of local folklore is a field that should by no means be neglected by historical organizations.

If you read Mason's first paragraph closely, you will note that it was written when the four media he mentioned were the only threats to the keeping of the folklore flame. Mason could not have conceived of how television and the Internet would redefine the collection and dissemination of folklore forever.

As this book was being written in the first year of the 21st century, it would have seemed that information overload may have left such dark and dusty notions such as folklore wallowing in its electronic wake. Quite to the contrary.

The electronic age–the "information superhighway" of television and technology instead seemed to have embraced the past.

Stories from previous books published by Exeter House Books were used as foundations for well-conceived programs for such cable television outlets as The History Channel, The Learning Channel, The Travel Channel, and even, in a mutated but important way, MTV.

Those networks realized quickly that ghost stories, mysteries, and secrets, are entertainment. People like a little "boo" in their lives, and if they pick up some serious historical facts along the way, so much the better.

There is a certain irony that as the World Wide Web and the cable television industries keep those flames of folklore and legend alive, some of the traditional places where one might expect those genres to thrive have snubbed them.

Historical societies and libraries too often give short shrift to folklore, and especially *ghostly* folklore. The stories are there, scattered throughout vertical files and deep within passages in books and newspapers. But, few have bothered to gather them and group them into viable and valuable collections of local lore.

This is not an indictment of those repositories. They have other things to do, other things to collect, other agendas to advance. Ghost stories, if they rise at all, rise only around Halloween.

I believe I can qualify all of what I just wrote by assuring the reader that I have served as president of the board of one of the largest public libraries in Pennsylvania and, for more than 20 years, have been on the board of one of the largest historical societies in the state. I am not being critical, just honest.

I am also sincere in my hopes that this simple book be embraced by those institutions–but moreover by the people of Chester County and the Brandywine Valley as an effort to keep those fires of folklore burning brightly.

This book also closes another gap.

This book, my 20th on ghosts and legends in the mid-Atlantic States, will encompass an area hitherto unexplored in those other efforts.

First, for the uninitiated, allow me to define the geographic parameters of this book.

It is *Ghost Stories of Chester County and the Brandywine Valley*.

As defined in tourism terms, the Brandywine Valley wraps around the Brandywine Creek and extends through Chester and Delaware counties in Pennsylvania.

It is a historically rich region that stretches from the Schuylkill River in the north to the Delaware River, Mason-Dixon Line and beyond the "New Castle Circle" that separates Pennsylvania and Delaware.

Geographics aside, it is the wellspring of Pennsylvania. It is in Delaware County that Swedish settlers became the first Europeans to establish homesteads in what would become Pennsylvania and where William Penn first set foot on the soil of his colony.

But it was well before those historic events that the roots of the supernatural took hold in this storied land.

Throughout this book, I will attempt to mix a bit of history, folklore, and legend along with the ghostly

3

tales of private homes, hotels, and business places in Chester County and beyond.

But allow me, please, to begin with a bit of explanation.

In an online booksellers' reader's review of one of my previous books, *Bucks County Ghost Stories,* an individual noted their disappointment with that volume, citing one factor: *"It seems as if ghosts in Bucks County tend to haunt mostly businesses that stand to benefit from being labeled as haunted."*

I wanted to at once mock and mourn that reader's assessment. I now have a chance to do both.

I will start by going back a few volumes before the Bucks County book to cite an example of how I would explain the world of ghost story collecting to that "reviewer."

I will cite my experience in Cape May, N.J.

The charming Victorian city on the southern tip of New Jersey just, well, *looks* haunted. Its gingerbread homes and gaslit, tree-shaded streets seem to be veritable breeding grounds of ghostly activity.

The decision to investigate the ghost stories in Cape May was a "no brainer." And, as it is known for its quaint bed and breakfasts and inns, those places were the logical places to begin.

Along the way, leads were received and led to private homes where spirits dwelled, but in nearly every one of those cases the property owners did not want their addresses or, many times, their real names used in the stories.

Trading anonymity for a story was nothing new to my research partners and me. One consideration in that regard, however, was the fact that readers could never actually visit those private properties, attempt to learn more about them, and perhaps have an encounter with their ghostly inhabitants.

4

Those B&Bs, restaurants, and inns in Cape May were, on the other hand, quite accessible. And, as our research efforts broadened, we discovered that many of the commercial properties were inhabited by ethereal entities.

An odd thing happened as we began to compile the ghost story leads from those B&Bs of Cape May.

Here's a graphic example using arbitrary figures.

If we went to 25 B&Bs and asked if they had any stories of hauntings, perhaps 15 said "yes."

Of those 15, however, perhaps eight said they did not want their ghost stories published in a book. *"It would be **bad for business**,"* they maintained.

The other seven had no problem with relating their experiences for any and all to read.

So, those B&Bs and their ghosts were included in *Cape May Ghost Stories, Book One.*

It wasn't too very long after the publication of what turned out to be a very successful book that two or three of those B&Bs that declined to release their stories called.

"How come you didn't use our story," they asked.

*"Because you said it would be **bad for business** and didn't want it used,"* I replied.

But what those businesses saw was that after the book reached the readers, many of those readers came to stay or dine in the establishments that allowed their stories to be told.

The ghost stories were, in the main, **good for business**.

There was, of course, a second Cape May Ghost Stories book, and some of those first-time holdouts relented and related their stories for all to read.

So yes, online reviewer, quite often "haunted" businesses do stand to benefit from the publicity.

But here's the reality. Here's why any sensitive and sensible reader would understand quickly exactly why so many B&Bs, hotels, taverns, inns, and historic sites just seem to have ghost stories to tell and why they appear in ghost story books across the world. Nowhere, anywhere, is it more obvious than in places such as Cape May, Bucks County–or the Brandywine Valley.

First, the reader should have a deep appreciation for this reality.

It is to the eternal credit of the B&B, hotel, tavern, inn, and historical society that they have lovingly, faithfully, and often *expensively* restored, refurbished, and reopened their properties as public places.

Throughout Chester and surrounding counties are hundreds of examples of ancient, historic buildings that have been maintained or rescued and used for commercial purposes.

And, in many of those structures, the ghosts came along for the restoration ride.

It is in those places that the reader of this kind of book can enjoy a meal in a haunted dining room or (try to) sleep in a haunted guest room or look over their shoulders for ghosts as they stroll through haunted corridors of a historic property.

And, if the owners or operators make a few bucks out of it, well, so be it. They pay nothing to be in the book, we pay nothing for their stories.

Having investigated and written about haunted places in many states and countries through more than two decades, I have watched as bits of history–and often *haunted* history–are destroyed and demolished. It sickens me sometimes.

To cite another tale, I take you to my native county, Berks. Not atypical of any other county in southeastern Pennsylvania, Berks has been victimized by rampant development and growth in recent years.

Left in the wake of that too often have been historic or locally significant places that have been razed for a

6

convenience store, mall, fast-food joint or gas station. A map of Berks County, and Chester County as well, is dotted and scarred by this kind of "progress."

So, to the innkeeper, restaurateur, or raconteur who spends money, time, and love to save a 200-year old hotel from the wrecker's ball or spare a 150-year old mansion and convert it to a B&B–thank you!

Thank you on behalf of this writer, those readers who just might drop by, and thanks mostly on behalf of the spirits for whom you have provided a comfortable habitat.

Charles J. Adams III
2001

The "Ticking Tombstone Church"

THE TICKING TOMBSTONE

There is one story that rises to the surface every time at the mere mention of ghosts and hauntings in Chester County.

Ask any countian who has kept aware of local lore about ghosts, and they're likely to know of one story that has somehow lingered in their memory.

It is the story of the ticking tombstone in the graveyard of the London Tract Meeting House near Stricklersville, London Britain Township.

The story has been bandied about on the edge of history for decades. In the early 1970s, the Pennsylva-

8

nia tourism office published a listing of a handful of haunted places in the state–and the ticking tombstone tale was on that list.

Built in 1729 and known originally as the Welsh Baptist Meeting, the building is now on the grounds of the White Clay Creek Preserve, a 1,253-acre conservation area administered by the Pennsylvania Bureau of State Parks.

It is just inside the Pennsylvania state line, just northwest of the "New Castle Circle" arc that forms the Pennsylvania/Delaware border and near "The Wedge" where those two states and Maryland meet awkwardly.

The old meeting house and its adjacent burial ground are eerie settings for a good ghost story. And, within the walls of the burial ground, there *is* one.

Not far from the meeting house is the Mason-Dixon Line, the 365-mile long boundary surveyed in 1767 by Charles Mason and Jeremiah Dixon, a pair of British mathematicians and astronomers hired to settle a land dispute between Pennsylvania and Maryland.

They did just that, but soon after they returned to work at the Royal Observatory, the line they left became a divider not only of two states, but of two sociopolitical philosophies. The Mason-Dixon Line came to divide the North from the South and, later, the nation.

It was not, of course, Messrs. Mason and Dixon's intent. They were just doing their job, and fighting myriad diversities doing it.

And interestingly, as they were doing that job, some locals couldn't figure out what that job might be. With their odd equipment and their stargazing, rumors circulated that they were practicing sorcery or, worse, necromancy.

But, they were *just doing their job*.

9

The story of the "ticking tombstone" has its genesis in Mason and Dixon's era.

It has long been held that a worker on the surveying and marking team was given (or stole) Jeremiah Dixon's pocket watch (or chronometer). At some point during the project, the worker took ill and died (or was murdered) and was buried in the London Tract graveyard.

His remains are beneath a weatherworn marble slab with the initials "R.C." only barely visible. As a point of reference, it is next to the oldest tombstone in the cemetery, a heart-shaped marker under which John Devon (d. March 8, 1735) is buried.

It is from within "R.C.'s" grave that the faint but distinct *tick...tick...tick* of Dixon's chronometer echoes eternally.

While that is the most popular version of the story, there is another. The ticking remains a constant, but the identification of the *tickee* changes in that second version.

The alternate tale maintains that the individual who swallowed the timepiece was an infant, who did so accidentally. And, that timepiece was *Mason's* pocket watch.

Despite efforts to retrieve the watch, and despite a wait for it to, well, pass, the device remained in the baby's belly for the rest of its 60-year life–and continues to tick to this very day.

Bill Morton, manager of the White Clay Creek Preserve, is well aware of the story set in the graveyard of the former meeting house that now serves as an environmental center.

"Locals call it the 'Ticking Tomb Church,'" he said.

Morton said there are still people who stop by to have a look and a listen. "I've been dumb enough to

10

bend down a listen for it too," Morton said. "But I've never heard it."

He considers the story an interesting bit of lore in the sprawling preserve.

The "Ticking Tombstone" (foreground)

11

"And," he added, "I suppose some people in the past must have heard the ticking, or the legend wouldn't have come down over the years."

The "ticking tombstone" is not the only strange tale in the area that was once destined to be submerged as part of a flood control reservoir.

Near the old meeting house was once an Indian village named Opasiskunk, or Minguannan. A recurring story in the area tells of a ghostly Indian maiden who has been seen gliding across the landscape on misty, moonlit nights.

And, there's Brigadoon-like legend that is also attributed to a glen within the present boundaries of the White Clay Creek Preserve.

It is said that a phantom church appears whenever a winter's fog envelops the land. Faintly, ever so faintly, the distinct outline of the church—what church, the legend fails to say—can be seen. And, just as one's eyes fix on its silhouette, it seems to sink into the soil.

One extension of that story is that the church appears and disappears in the aforementioned fashion only once every 100 years.

Does that church rise and vanish on foggy nights? Stand by that old graveyard on a foggy night and find out.

Does a ghostly Indian maiden stroll a nearby meadow? Keep an eye out for her.

And does the old chronometer in "R.C.'s" belly still *tick...tick...tick* from the grave? Visit it, cock an ear, and listen closely.

📖

The statue of General Anthony Wayne at Valley Forge

BOILED FLESH, LOST BONES, AND THE GHOST OF "MAD ANTHONY"

Perhaps no place in the world has a ghost story quite like this one.

This is a book of collected legends and investigated hauntings in the Brandywine Valley, which, as I explained earlier, encompasses Chester and Delaware counties in Pennsylvania.

But this ghost wanders far beyond the bounds of this enchanted area of southeastern Pennsylvania. In fact, it might be spotted anywhere from Paoli to Port Matilda; Malvern to Meadville.

13

This is a story of flesh boiled in a cauldron, misplaced bones, and an American hero who is buried in two graves–about 400 miles apart!

First, a bit about that American hero.

His grandfather emigrated from Ireland and settled near Paoli in 1720. There, at the family's homestead, he was born on the first day of 1745.

As a child, he was known to "play army" with friends. A schoolmaster told the boy's father that the boy was "certainly not a scholar, perhaps a soldier." Still, he learned enough to become a successful surveyor.

He inherited his father's estate in 1775 and plunged himself into the struggle for American independence. In January, 1776, he was appointed as a colonel in the 4th Pennsylvania Battalion.

Col. Anthony Wayne.

The triumphs and travails of his military career fill pages of history books. His legacy remains in the names of counties, towns, and townships across America.

That name has been expanded in popular usage to "Mad" Anthony Wayne, a sobriquet said to have been given to Wayne by one of his soldiers who marveled at his commander's impetuous, zealous personality.

So cunning was "Mad Anthony" that, at the time of his death, he was the ranking office in the United States Army.

Gen. Wayne's career was actually on the upswing in 1796. He had been on his way home from successful campaigns and the surrender of the British forces in the Great Lakes region (considered by some historians to be the final chapter of the American Revolution) when he took ill aboard a ship bound for the port of Presque Isle, now Erie, Pennsylvania.

14

Stricken with gout, Gen. Wayne was taken to the blockhouse on Presque Isle. A friend and Army surgeon, Dr. James C. Wallace, had been beckoned to the general's side, but he arrived too late. On December 15, 1796, "Mad Anthony" died.

It was upon his death that a bizarre legend was born.

Actually, the legend is rooted in fact–almost unfathomable and certainly quite grisly fact.

On his deathbed, Gen. Wayne had given instructions that he be buried in full dress uniform, polished boots, and in a simple pine coffin at the base of the flagstaff at the blockhouse.

His wish was granted.

For 13 years, the general's body rested in that grave. But in the spring of 1809, Anthony Wayne's son, Isaac, journeyed from the family estate in Chester County. His mission was to retrieve his father's remains and return them to be reinterred "back home."

Himself a colonel in the army, Isaac Wayne engaged the aforementioned Dr. Wallace to exhume the body and prepare it for transport.

Historians can only speculate on the reasons for what happened next.

In his 1896 *Biographical Dictionary and Historical Reference Book of Erie County, Pennsylvania*, S.B. Nelson provided a chilling account:

> On opening the grave, all present were amazed to find the body petrified, with the exception of one foot and leg, which were partially gone. The boot on the unsound leg had decayed and most of the clothing was missing.
>
> Dr. Wallace separated the body into convenient parts and placed them in a kettle of boiling water until the flesh could be removed from the bones.

Old Blockhouse — "Mad Anthony" Wayne Monument, Erie, Pa.

A ca. 1905 view of the Presque Isle Blockhouse

16

Then, he carefully scraped the bones, packed them in a small box, and returned the flesh, with the implements used in the operation, to the coffin, which had been left undisturbed, and it was again covered over with earth.

The box was secured to Col. Wayne's sulky and carried to Eastern Pennsylvania.

Why was this almost ghoulish act undertaken? Why was Gen. Wayne's body dismembered and its flesh boiled from its bones?

Nelson believed it was done to reduce the remains to their most compact form to fit in the short buckboard used for the cross-state transport. There is another theory that the procedure was adapted from an ancient Indian custom.

There is also the story, not mentioned in Nelson's Erie County history, that a dispute arose between the general's Chester County son—who wanted his father reburied in the family plot—and officials in Erie, who insisted the remains remain at Presque Isle.

Nelson did address that with an adroit observation:

Col. Wayne is reported to have said, in regard to the affair: 'I always regretted it; had I known the state of the remains were in before separated I think I should certainly have had them again deposited there and let them rest, and had a monument erected to his memory.

That, of course, was not done. The colonel packed his dad's bones in the buggy and went over several rivers and through many woods back to Chester County. His course was a road that roughly parallels the present U.S. Route 322.

On July 4, 1809, what was left of "Mad Anthony" Wayne's bones were buried in the graveyard of St. David's Church in Radnor.

17

The result, of course, is the reality that the good general is among the very few individuals in history to have his flesh buried one place and his bones buried at another.

It was that journey across Pennsylvania that sparked the unsettling tales of the unsettled ghost of "Mad Anthony."

In its official web site, Erie County provides an eerie account of its version of the ghost story. There, it is said, Wayne's headless spirit prowls the streets of town in search of its head, which was, according to *tourerie.com*, "inconveniently buried separately from his body."

Another story from the northwestern panhandle of Pennsylvania claims that it is upon horseback that the ghost of the general–head and all–wanders the area around the blockhouse (an 1880 reproduction of the original) on Presque Isle around midnight each night.

But, there's more...much more.

It seems that along the way from Erie to Radnor, a few of our hero's bones–and perhaps, *just perhaps* his very skull–were clunked from the carriage as it rattled along the rocky, rutted, and muddied road.

To this day, when the conditions are right, "Mad Anthony's" ghost can be seen searching for whatever limb, rib, or–perhaps, *just perhaps*, skull–it might collect on its eternal sojourn.

The general's spirit is said to cross Chester County on a course roughly along routes 30 and 322, and is likely to be seen at any time, any place. Most likely, "Mad Anthony" will be seen on his favorite horse, "Nag," who will also appear in ghostly form.

Not only does Gen. Wayne have the singular distinction of being buried in two places; his ghost has to rank among the most rambunctious in the world.

18

It seems that his spirit has been reported rambling through Storm King Pass along the Hudson River (recreating a ride he made there warning Colonial troops about British army movements); seated near the fireplace in the dining room of the commandant's house at Ft. Ticonderoga, N.Y. (which he once commanded); within the ruins of the Philip Noland farm in Loudoun County, Virginia (he and Noland were good friends and Wayne visited there often); and in Indian scout's garb along Lake Memphremagog, Vermont (for no apparent reason).

But, in its purest form, the legend holds that it is New Year's morning each year that the general's ghost rises from its grave in the St. David's Churchyard to begin its lonely and long journey to Erie and back.

This, then, leads us to our next "Mad Anthony"-related haunting–Waynesborough.

As anyone in the area knows, Waynesborough is not a town, but a fine Georgian fieldstone farmhouse just south of Paoli.

The home has had its share of intrigue. On one occasion, British troops descended on the property, intent on capturing Wayne for questioning of his loyalty to the Crown. It is said they ransacked several rooms before being chased away by Polly Wayne, the future general's wife.

Believing Anthony might have hidden in boxwoods to the rear of the property, the Red Coats attacked the shrubs and found nobody. Those boxwoods are still a part of the lush landscaping at Waynesborough.

While there is little documentation, it is believed the west wing of the home was built in 1724 on 1,600 acres of Wayne family land. The central portion of the home went up in 1735 and an east wing, called the "new kitchen," was added in 1792. A second floor was added to that new wing in 1860 and several other modifications were made in ensuing years.

The Wayne homestead went through tough times (in 1835, the family unsuccessfully tried to sell it to raise quick cash), and in 1965 it fell into the hands of Orrin Wickersham June, a New York architect who returned the home to an early 19th-century appearance.

Despite his extensive and expensive renovations, June's wife, a Wayne descendent, chose not to live in the home and the property was eventually turned over to the county for historic preservation. The home, where the likes of Ben Franklin, Alexander Hamilton, James Madison, and the Marquis de Lafayette have visited, was added to the National Register of Historic Places in 1973.

It was added to the register of *haunted* places long before that.

In fact, it was during the June family's occupancy, according to historian Bob Goshorn, that the legendary ghost of Waynesborough first reared its raucous head and may have chased Mrs. June away.

Orrin June was hosting a dinner party when something quite odd and unexpected happened.

As the couples gathered around the table chatted, every woman present raised her arms in surprise and some mumbled or shrieked.

The female members of the staff likewise expressed instant horror.

The men at the table and in the service staff were silenced and shocked at the women's sudden, inexplicable reaction.

It seemed that every woman, but no man, had heard what was described as a "terrible crashing of glass" coming from somewhere in the house.

"Mad Anthony's" grave at St. David's

21

As the men sat confused and the women sat cowering in confusion, yet another blast of glass-shattering was heard—only by the females!

The incident sent shivers of fear through the women. The men sat mute.

Mr. June reportedly mentioned the bizarre incident to a previous occupant of the house, and he confirmed that it had happened before.

It was explained that the source of the glass-shattering sound is the ghost of Hannah Wayne, a family member who resided and died in the house in the mid-1800s.

Hannah was alone in the house one day. All the other women of the manor were in the nearby garden and the men were in distant fields.

Hannah was going about her chores, climbing through a trap door into the attic. Somehow, she was literally trapped in the trap door. She struggled to free herself, but in the process knocked over a candle that ignited her dress.

In utter panic, Hannah freed herself and struggled toward the nearest window. In a fiery frenzy, she managed to kick the window out and scream. But, it was too late. Moments later, the flames consumed her.

It is said the women in the gardens heard Hannah's death scream and heard the window shattering. The men, farther away in the fields, heard nothing.

It is also said that to this day, that muffled scream and the shattering glass sound can still be heard—only, of course, by women!

An article in the October, 1997, *Main Line Today* magazine reported that the site manager at the time did confirm that she had been rudely awakened one night by the sound of crashing glass and a sobbing sound coming from the attic. Her husband had heard nothing.

However, Sesilie Oehler, who with her husband, Lance, are caretakers at Waynesborough, minimized the incident, and said their seven years there have been "pretty quiet."

Waynesborough at the turn of the 20th century (top), and 100 years later

23

Site of the Paoli Massacre

THE GUILTY GHOST OF PAOLI

A few miles west from where Gen. Anthony Wayne was born and (most of him) is buried is where "Mad Anthony" and perhaps the entire Continental Army, suffered their most humiliating encounters of the Revolutionary War.

Around midnight, September 20, 1777, American troops under Gen. Wayne's command were confronted by British soldiers in a field near what is now Malvern.

The British were ordered to strike silently and swiftly, so with bayonets affixed and no shots fired, they surprised the slumbering Colonials and killed 53 of them in what history has recorded as the "Paoli Massacre."

Total American wounded numbered more than 300 and the British suffered only four casualties.

The attack, and Wayne's alleged negligence in camping his troops so close to British lines, led to charges of military blundering against him. The general requested and received a court martial, which cleared him of the charges.

At the site of the Paoli Massacre today are several monuments set in a municipal park. The centerpiece of the memorials is a six-foot obelisk erected in 1817. Its etched words have been worn smooth by time and weather.

It stands in the middle of a cemetery in which the 53 fallen soldiers are buried. Following the "massacre," local farmers collected the corpses and placed them in a common grave. A wall which surrounds the small graveyard contains field stones taken from the Ezekiel Brown cabin, one of several in which the American soldiers were camped when the attack occurred.

On another monument there, an account of the attack accuses the British of "cold-blooded cruelty" and "barbarity" in the "atrocious massacre." Conversely, it characterizes the hometown hero, Gen. Wayne, as an officer whose "bravery and humanity were equally conspicuous."

What these monuments do not mark is the course of the midnight ride of the ghost of the Paoli massacre.

Long talked about by even the most respected local citizens, the ghost is that of a victim of the Paoli Massacre–perhaps the last American victim–who is doomed to ride silently at midnight on the anniversary of the tragedy.

Some say the ghostly soldier and steed can be seen on nights other than September 20, and everyone who has reported its presence says the same thing.

The faint image of a sturdy white horse emerges as if from a mist. Riding atop it is a blue-uniformed soldier.

Two things will strike as being odd, should you see this ghost.

There is no sound.

There is no head.

This particular soldier was a local fellow. And, in order to spend as much time as he could with his wife and, he claimed, save the troops a ration or two, he requested and received permission to go to his home after his soldiering duties were done each day.

If he didn't have a watch, he would be given a pass to stay overnight at his home. One night, however, he had a terrible dream. In that dream, his encampment down the road was being attacked by the Redcoats.

He managed to shake off the nightmare, roll over, and go back to sleep. But within minutes, the vision came back to him.

In a sweaty panic, he leaped out of bed, hurriedly put on his uniform and, despite his wife's protestations, mounted his white horse and galloped back to camp.

With campfires casting an eerie glow on the grounds, he looked across his camp with horror. All he could see was battered, beaten, and bruised men. All he could hear were the moaning, groaning sounds of agony. All he could smell was the stench of death.

At once, he heard a rustling sound. It was a British soldier, running from the nearby underbrush. The Colonial trooper jerked around and looked up to see his adversary's sword gleaming in the moonlight.

That sword came down in a frightful blur, taking the young American's head with it!

It is this headless horseman of the Paoli Massacre who, still today, rides silently and aimlessly from the battle grounds to and through nearby neighborhoods.

Anyone who may come across this Paoli ghost should beware, they say. If you see him and follow him too closely, he may whirl around and thrust his bloody, severed head your way. According to the legend, should this happen to you, you will not live to see another birthday!

Is this all just the stuff of campfire tales? Just a scary old story?

Not long ago, a prominent local doctor, former Tredyffrin Township school director, and member of one of the most prominent families in the area said he saw the headless ghost several times.

He always kept his distance!

The Octoraro Hotel, around 1906

OCTORARO EDDIE

"Things happen here that we can't explain," she said.

"You'll see a shadow here and there and swear that a person just passed by."

She is Cindy McAneny, owner of the historic Octoraro Hotel at 2 S. 3rd St. in Oxford. And, she is one of several persons who believe the hotel is haunted.

Whenever lights flicker on and off, whenever doors creak open or slam shut on their own, they blame it on the resident ghost.

They've come to call that ghost "Eddie."

After a fire in the hotel in the late 1990s, Cindy's brother stayed there alone in a third floor room. "Every night," Cindy said, "he would hear somebody walk down the hallway and into a room. But, there was never anybody else up there."

Doors could clearly be heard opening and closing. Footsteps would clunk down darkened halls. A thorough check would reveal nothing, nobody.

Built in 1827 as a stagecoach stop, the hotel has seen its share of travelers and locals who have spun many a yarn within its walls.

Bo Bigley, whose has worked as a cook at the hotel for many years, claimed, "The basement seems to have a personality."

More than that, she added, the kitchen and a hallway that leads to it seem to be the center for much unexplained activity.

"Sometimes when I'm in the kitchen," she continued, "I'll see something in the corner of my eye.

I'll turn around and I'll see a gentleman standing there, in 19th century dress."

Bo described the chap as wearing a dark gray jacket, a high collar, and a top hat.

"He's very tall," she added. "I've seen him off and on."

"It looks as if he could step right out and get into his horse and buggy at any time," she said.

Although she is convinced–or has convinced herself–that whatever spirits dwell in the Octoraro Hotel are benevolent, Cindy McAneny was visibly nervous when she said, "People live in this building–and we don't know who they are."

THE PHANTOM HITCHHIKER
OF THE PENNSYLVANIA TURNPIKE

The mysterious 1972 disappearance and subsequent Pennsylvania Turnpike road death of lounge singer Jerome Alch touched off a mystery that spilled over several counties of southeastern Pennsylvania and dipped deeply into the realm of the unexplained.

The West Chester *Local News* front-paged a story about reports of bizarre happenings on the superhighway–happenings that took place near the spot where workmen discovered the body of the 37-year old Philadelphian on February 5.

Alch had been reported missing from an engagement at the Plaza Madrid, a Reading nightclub.

Alch's body and the wreck of his car were found in the icy waters of the Marsh Creek in Upper Uwchlan Township, near the Downingtown Interchange of the turnpike. Officials theorized he was killed in a violent one-car crash the night of his reported disappearance, and thick underbrush had concealed the wreckage and body for a full three weeks until the discovery.

During those three weeks, there were at least a dozen reports of ghostly sightings and occurrences that took place between the Downingtown and Morgantown interchanges, according to the West Chester newspaper.

Motorists observed a spectral hitchhiker along the turnpike, and those who were brave enough to pick him up were warned of the imminent end of the world. Just as mysteriously as he appeared, they claimed, he disappeared!

Similar reports in other locales have been publicized at other times, and most fall into the deep bin of folklore known as the "urban legend."

But, motorists interviewed at the time steadfastly denied they had ever heard similar stories and insisted that what they experienced was the absolute truth.

In fact, the ghostly reports were actually given before Alch's body was found. Up until the discovery of the wreck, nobody had any ideas as to his whereabouts.

Although many more tales of the supernatural happenings were told after the finding of the body–and therefore subject to suspicion–many people naively told their tales and said they knew nothing of the Jerome Alch saga. One woman said she nearly hit a medial strip when she turned around to see who was tapping on her shoulder while she was driving–alone!

Others reported an apparently distraught man standing along the turnpike with hands outstretched toward the heavens. As they drove closer, he faded into the night.

Turnpike toll-takers and police were skeptical, but the stories circulated for months nonetheless.

Reporter Shirley Macauley wrote in the *Local News*, "Perhaps the phantom hitchhiker was the spirit of a man unable to accept the sudden fact of his own death, that he appeared along the roadside seeking help, discovery, confirmation, and that 'end of the world' he is supposed to have predicted was the end not of the entire world, but of his own."

📖

"SANDY FLASH,"
THE ROGUE OF DOE RUN

As our research team canvassed the handsome borough of Kennett Square—popping into shops, taverns, and the fine Bayard Taylor Memorial Library, we almost *gave up* the ghost because there were no ghosts to be found on the busy streets of the town.

Later, as our search broadened, we would find them. First, though, as we pored through books and historical documents at the library, we found the bizarre tale of local legend "Sandy Flash."

The name was adapted by noted writer and Kennett Square native Bayard Taylor and the character was fashioned after James Fitzpatrick, a West Marlborough Township man who was a blacksmith by vocation and a rogue by reputation.

Fitzpatrick was said to have been a strapping, impetuous young man who would gallop by on his horse in what one contemporary in his home village of Doe Run called a "sandy flash"—his long red hair flowing in the wind. Hence, his nickname.

Although he joined the Continental Army at the outbreak of the Revolutionary War and was wounded in battle in 1777, he eventually deserted, was captured, was imprisoned, was released, deserted again, was imprisoned again, escaped, was captured again and imprisoned again, and escaped once more.

In a daring series of events, Fitzpatrick made his way through the Chester County countryside and joined the army again–this time, the British army. He served as a guide and scout for the Redcoats at the Battle of Brandywine and was rewarded by the British for his efforts.

But, as the tide of battle turned and the British evacuated Philadelphia, James Fitzpatrick became a man without a country. Folks in Chester and surrounding counties knew he had raided local farms to secure supplies and food for the King's army. So, when he returned to the sparsely settled countryside around Doe Run, he was at once feared and reviled.

He took to wearing disguises and took to the roads as a bandit. All the while, Colonial authorities had placed a bounty on his head. "Sandy Flash," the turncoat, would be captured, tried, and executed for his crimes against his countrymen.

On August 22, 1778, the man who was described in a newspaper of the day as "the celebrated bandit of Chester County" was found and taken into custody. He was imprisoned in Chester, but that lockup proved too frail.

He nearly escaped.

So, he was remanded to a larger prison in Philadelphia, but that lockup proved too frail.

He nearly escaped–twice!

Sandy Flash reached the end of his rope–so to speak–on September 26, 1778, when he was hanged at the corner of Providence and Edgemont in Chester.

But, Sandy Flash didn't go down without a final fight. He didn't exactly reach the end of that rope.

He nearly escaped death.

The "celebrated bandit" was positioned atop a flatbed wagon with the noose around his neck. When the wagon was pulled from under him, he would drop. The noose, of course, would tighten and he would die.

But, the rope was a bit too long. When the wagon was pulled away, Sandy Flash dropped–but not far enough. He was able to break his fall by landing on his tiptoes. There, he eased the strain on his neck and staved off death.

Aghast, the executioner was forced to place his weight on Sandy's shoulders to force him down and finish the deed.

Of all the legends that have grown around Sandy Flash over the centuries, two remain tantalizing.

It is said that the highwayman buried large sums of gold, silver, and jewels that he gathered in his exploits throughout the Chester County countryside.

And, somewhere, some say, the bandit's booty remains buried and awaiting discovery.

Old Sandy himself may not have completed his mad dashes across the Brandywine Valley.

His ghost is said to still wander from village to village, tavern to tavern, a haunting highwayman in search of mortals to victimize with the echoing thunder of a horse's hooves and a stiff rush of cold wind as he flashes by in an eternal gallop.

The Kennett Square Inn

LETITIA, THE GHOST OF THE KENNETT SQUARE INN

A landmark at 201 E. State Street in Kennett Square is the Kennett Square Inn.

Built in 1835 as a private residence, the building underwent its first major expansion just after the Civil War.

In 1927, it was known as the Green Gate Tea Room, and in 1933, after Prohibition was repealed, it became a tavern.

Its present configuration took shape in 1976.

Steve Warner has owned the Kennett Square Inn since then, and since then has lived with the ghosts that wander freely through the corridors and chambers of the lovely fine-dining establishment.

"We gave the ghost a name," he said. "We call her Letitia."

The name is purely arbitrary, and was pulled out of the historical hat.

In 1699, William Penn set thousands of acres aside for his son, William Jr., and daughter, Letitia. That acreage included most of what is now Kennett Square. The sprawling land grant took the name "Letitia's Manor" until it was carved into lots and one of those lots became known as Kennett–after a village in Wiltshire, England.

Thus, it is somewhat fitting and proper that the memory of Letitia Penn–if only nebulously–lives on at the Kennett Square Inn.

Steven Ward has grown comfortable with the ghost or ghosts that are within the walls of the elegant dining room and tavern.

"I've been here 19 years," he said, "and I used to live upstairs. I was told by a chef who also lived there that during days and evenings things would fall off shelves and then spin around the floor."

It wasn't long until Steve had his own encounters with the pesky poltergeists.

"One time when I was sleeping upstairs, I felt a darkness come through my room. It got very dark," he remembered.

And, as he lay there trying to sleep and trying to reckon with the "darkness within darkness" that swept into his bedchamber, things got, as they say, weird.

"It got very cold in the room," he continued. "And all of a sudden I felt the bed jumping up and down by my feet! It was as if someone was jumping at the end of the bed."

Steve Ward is a rational, sensible man not prone to hysteria. But the incident that night in an upstairs room at the inn left him forever changed.

"I was petrified. I thought someone was in the room. I didn't move. And then...this thing left the room–and that was the end of that."

It was the end of *that*–but not the end of ghostly sightings in the building.

Some employees and customers have reported unexplainable phenomena in the Kennett Square Inn. Steve remembered one in particular.

"I had a couple here one time come in for dinner. They came in early, just before a party we were setting up for. They were the only ones in the dining room.

"They got up and paid their check and left. And then, the party came in, we got very busy," he said.

What happened next was something he wasn't prepared for, in more ways than one.

"We got a phone call. They wanted to speak to the manager. It was the woman who had been here earlier, having dinner.

"She was nervous, she said, the whole way home. She felt she had to talk to someone. She hadn't mentioned anything to her husband, thinking he would think she was nuts.

"Well, she asked me if we had any ghosts in the restaurant."

Although a party was unfolding all around him, Steve listened patiently and raptly to the woman as she explained why she asked that question.

"She said that while they were having dinner, she constantly felt someone over her shoulder. She said that she kept looking around and there was no one else in the dining room at the time.

"Her husband got up from the table to go to the bathroom. She watched him leave the room. She turned around, looked back to where her husband had been sitting.

"She said she saw, sitting where her husband had been sitting, a young girl. She said the girl was dressed in Colonial-style garb. She said the girl looked to be about 13 years old.

"The woman looked over to see if her husband was coming back in. Then, she looked back at the chair and the girl was gone!"

Steve listened patiently to the woman, and invited her back to the inn to go over historical documents related to the property. He was convinced that the caller was telling him the truth about her experience.

A shaking bed, a phantom diner, and other potentially frightening encounters aside, one particular incident stands out in Steve Warner's mind. In that incident, even the borough police became involved.

"One time," he remembered, "the police called me at home at five o'clock in the morning. They said someone was locked inside the restaurant. I had to go there and open up.

"Now, we have a motion detector and the alarm goes off. But, the cops said somebody called them from the payphone in the restaurant.

"They said they called the police station and the police traced it back to the Kennett Square Inn.

"Well," Steve continued, "I went in. We searched the whole building and there was nobody here. The building was totally secure, dead-bolted.

"But something was going on, we just didn't know what."

And, perhaps the mysteries of the Kennett Square Inn will never really be explained.

39

THE DORLAN DEVIL

A minor wave of hysteria swept through Upper Uwchlan Township in the 1930s when a creature that came to be known as the "Dorlan Devil" reared its ugly head on at least two occasions.

In 1932, two nurserymen were working in the area just north of Dorlan when they were approached by a leaping being they described as "neither beast nor human."

Both men assured the many skeptics that they were familiar with every known wild animal, and what they saw was nothing like anything they'd ever seen before.

Although a search party was mounted and swept through the surrounding countryside, nothing was sighted or tracked. The creature left no prints and no clues as to from where it came or where it went.

Interestingly, the Dorlan sighting came during a spate of far-flung sightings of a legendary monster from the dunes and Pine Barrens of the Garden State–the "Jersey Devil."

In their book *The Jersey Devil*, authors James F. McGloy and Ray Miller Jr. mentioned the 1932 Dorlan sighting. And, they recalled two other sightings in the region in January, 1909.

One was in Chester, where an eyewitness described an odd creature that flung itself from a railroad boxcar and dashed into the darkness.

The other was in Leiperville, where a gent named Daniel Flynn told anyone who would listen that he spied a lightning-fast, six-foot tall "thing" that had skin like an alligator. It, too, fled swiftly into the night.

As for the "Dorlan Devil," its second coming was in July, 1937, when the local papers bristled with an account from Downingtown mill worker Cydney Ladley, who encountered the monster while he, his wife, and another woman were motoring on the road from Dorlan to Milford Mills.

Ladley said what he saw was an "oversized kangaroo with long black hair and eyes like red saucers."

In the newspaper account, the writer further described the eyes as the kind that would "strike terror into your heart."

"They burn with a fiery intensity that seems to shrivel your soul," the article continued.

Ladley, his testimony backed up fully by the woman who accompanied him on the fateful night, said the beast took a giant leap across the roadway in one bound and disappeared into a swamp.

Upon his arrival home, Ladley put out the alarm to several neighbors and friends and about a dozen of same returned to that swampy area to search–in vain–for what the reporter said had returned "like a terrorizing apparition from the pre-historic past."

And what of this mysterious, elusive creature? Does the "Dorlan Devil" exist only in the faint and fading memories of the area's elders? Is it the stuff only of legend and lore?

Could the "devil" rise once more and send chills down the spine of the unaware in Upper Uwchlan? That's not likely.

That roadway where Cydney Ladley and company had their hair-raising experience is now deep beneath the waters of the Marsh Creek Lake.

But then again, who is to say that some day, or some night, someone may well see a preternatural

41

figure rise from those waters, breech, and plummet back into the depths?

Or, perhaps the "devil" may slither from the waves and wiggle onto the shore of the lake to show itself ever so briefly and mysteriously once more.

One never knows.

CAPTAIN KIDD'S TREASURE...
...IN CHESTER COUNTY?

Stories of caches and stashes of silver and gold, buried treasures, and hidden troves of jewels and gems are common in the folklore of the Brandywine Valley.

What could well be the most bizarre of all these tales has been told in the fields and forests near Honey Brook.

The account dates to the winter of 1895 when a reporter from a Philadelphia newspaper tracked down a story involving three local men who were bound and determined to discover a treasure chest that was said to be buried near what was called "Griffith's Clearing," near the Chester County town.

A. Scott Griffith was said to be a sensible, sane man, respected in business and church affairs. "One of Honey Brook's most valued citizens," one person said of him.

But one night, Mr. Griffith had a dream—a quite vivid dream.

He dreamed he saw a tree–a tree that was familiar to him. Within the soil beneath that tree, the dream told him, was an abundance of gold and glittering jewels.

For months, he dismissed the dream. He was a practical man and not prone to be moved to action or emotion by such sleep-induced fantasy.

Still, the thought lingered with him. In the fall of 1895, he revealed the contents of his dream to friend and local farmer Lorenzo Hackett. Then, and only then, would he be shocked into the realization that there might have been more to his dream than he could ever have imagined.

Hackett, himself a trusted member of the community, told Griffith that he, too, had dreamed of a treasure buried beneath a tree. As they compared notes, they discovered that both had envisioned the very same tree and the very same treasure.

Both agreed there was more substance than coincidence.

Griffith and Hackett decided to take their revelation to a third man, Budd Smith. A former iron miner, Smith was known to have certain strange powers–powers to find underground veins of ore and powers to "see things" that others could not. Smith was said to have "the gift."

Indeed, Smith boasted that he could "smell" the ore no matter how deep beneath the surface it may be.

This gifted man was intrigued by Griffith's and Hackett's dreams. As the three men talked, they gained one another's' confidences and mapped out a plan.

As the story goes, "Right after night one or all of the trio might be seen walking quietly towards Griffiths' meadow, armed with pick and shovel. It was a hard place to work and the work had to be done secretly, of course, or the whole county might come in and lay claim to a share of the treasure."

By the time the newspaperman paid a call to the secret excavation, it was "big enough to bury a couple of horses or to form the cellar of a small-sized house."

"The tree was the poet's typical 'sentinel,'" the writer continued. "It had but two big limbs, and these stood outward like arms pointing to the fence and guarding all beneath.

"Between these limbs the moonbeams played in fantastic figures, casting their shadows in and about the hole," he added.

Despite their nocturnal trudges and digging, the men were discovered by a handful of locals who pledged to keep their secret. But, one of the men who found out about the trio's efforts provided another element to this story that extended it far beyond the fields of Honey Brook into the high seas.

What that man added might have been the psychic source of Griffith's and Hackett's dreams and what drove them to their labors.

What they might have been digging for, though they could not have known by virtue of simple dreams, was the buried treasure of Captain Kidd.

Captain Kidd's treasure.

In Honey Brook Township, Chester County.

If that seems far beyond the bounds of just the bizarre, take into account the story told by that other man, whose name was not recorded by the reporter.

He said he had not long ago been fishing along the Brandywine Creek near Two Log Run when he came upon a small cabin and struck up a conversation with an old–very old–black woman he recalled being named Maria Collins.

She claimed to be about 108 years old, and in lucid terms she shared with the man certain facts and legends of the area.

"Somehow the conversation drifted towards pirates," the man told the writer. "And, the name of the famous Captain Kidd was mentioned.

"Then, the old woman told me that she had once heard her grandfather tell how Captain Kidd and his cutthroat crew had at one time been chased up the Brandywine. At that time, the stream was quite wide and deep and vessels of ordinary draught could come all the way up to here.

"Well, it seems that Captain Kidd was cruising off the Delaware capes when he saw a ship. He hailed her and found her to be a Spanish merchantman laden with gold and jewels and the rare old wines of the sunny lands."

Having learned that, the man continued, Captain Kidd and his mates boarded the Spanish ship, killed its crew, and offloaded the bounty onto their own ship.

"Hardly was the conquest over when an English man-of-war hove in sight and gave chase," the man added. "There was but one way for Kidd to run and that was up the Delaware. Naturally, the Britisher followed. Kidd's craft was fleet of sail, but the wily pirate knew he was going to be penned in sooner or later. There was only one chance, and that was to go up the Brandywine. Kidd's ship was light of draught and he got all the way up, but grounded on the calamus beds off Lenape."

The pirates hastened farther inland to make good their escape, but before departing the valley of the Brandywine, they did what all good buccaneers do–buried their ill-gotten loot deep in the ground, somewhere near Honey Brook.

The dreams of two men and the tale of one 108-year old black woman converged to make for a stirring story for readers of the newspaper back in December, 1895. But, the men eventually gave up their

46

search and shoveled dirt over their dreams, never to lay claim to Captain Kidd's treasure.

If it ever was really there at all.

•

The notion of buried treasures in the Brandywine Valley is not limited to Captain Kidd.

Some believe that Sandy Flash, the Doe Run ne'er-do-well, deposited some of his ill-gotten wealth somewhere between West Chester and Kennett Square.

And, it has long been held that Mother Nature herself has buried valuable ores just under the fertile soil of the region.

Consider a June, 1875 story in the Reading *Eagle* newspaper that documented a stir in the area around Warwick Furnace.

The headline read *IS IT THE CHARMED CIRCLE? IS IT MONEY, IRON ORE, OR WHAT?*

"The most wonderful excitement prevails in this neighborhood," the special correspondent began. "The old, middle aged and young are excited and trying to divine what the wonderful story means."

Rumors spread like wildfire around Warwick that abundant veins of silver could be found by anyone willing to take the time and effort to dig and discover them.

"The Indians used to dig the ore and smelt it," the writer continued, "and trade it off in pieces, weighing from three ounces to five pounds, for beads, tobacco and whisky."

The correspondent added that stories had long been told of the white settlers' attempts to find the natives' mineshafts, but with no success.

Within the story was an intriguing tale of an individual folks around Warwick may have encountered in the early years of the 19th century.

Indian Hannah.

47

The *Eagle* correspondent recorded the memories of a "Mrs. Quimby," who remembered Indian Hannah quite well.

"The children were afraid of her and looked upon her as a witch," Mrs. Quimby recalled. "She always came when the moon was very nearly full, slept in the barns in the neighborhood, and would steal out during the night and gather quartz."

Indian Hannah, said another Warwick resident, would carry her quartz in linen bags and sell it to a man named Isaac Pyle in Downingtown.

"Every effort was made by Pyle to induce this Indian woman to disclose where she found the ore," the story continued, "but she always replied that the secret would be buried with her."

And what of the "charmed circle," as mentioned in the headline?

That tale came from a young man named George Schick, who lived near the Warwick Furnace. When interviewed by the scribe, he provided an eerie account.

He told the writer that he was walking through a field (the exact location of which he declined to disclose) when he saw a well-dressed, middle-aged man.

"He was carrying a gold-headed cane," Schick told the reporter, "and he asked me to take a walk with him. I did not want to go, but I felt that I could not refuse him, so I walked with him.

"We made a large circle in the field, and after doing so, he stopped and said 'my boy, can you remember the circle we have made?'

"I told him that I could. 'Well,' he says, 'inside that circle is a deposit of great wealth.'

"He then described a small circle in one portion of the outer one, in which he stated there lays the great bulk of the wealth."

What happened then added even more intrigue to Schick's experience.

The lad said that after the stranger disclosed his circular secrets, the cane he was carrying suddenly broke into three pieces and vanished.

As did, in the next instant, the man!

*"Indian Hannah's" grave on the ground
of the Embreeville Complex.*

Indian Hannah, of course, was much more than the topic of casual conversation in Chester County. She is etched into county history as "the last Lenni Lenape"—a claim disputed by most rejected by some historians.

Hannah died March 20, 1802 in the poorhouse of Chester County.

You can pay last respects to Indian Hannah, if you can find her grave.

On the edge of a hardscrabble park, along a gravel lane, and next to a mulch dump on the grounds of the Embreeville Center along Route 162 is

a stone worn white and smooth by generations who
have paused to sit upon it.

"Here Rests Indian Hannah," a bronze plaque
states quite simply, "Last of the Lenni-Lenape Indians
in Chester County."

📖

THE SNOWBALL-THROWING GHOST

In the years just before and through the Civil War, a certain barn in Honey Brook Township figured in a sensational ghost story that spread far from that rolling, rural section of Chester County.

The location was given only as "up over the hill from Dampman's Station." The afflicted barn was that of Absolom Wilson. What happened there drew crowds from miles around.

It was the dead of winter, 1860, when Joseph Morrison, Wilson's nephew, made first contact with the energy in his uncle's barn.

Sometimes, a ghost manifests itself as an eerie glow...a milky white mist...a flash in the darkness...a so-called "orb" that appears in a photograph.

In this case, it was an orb of an altogether different kind.

In Joe Morrison's encounter, the spook made its presence known by hurling a snowball at the lad.

If this all sounds a little too cute and trite, please read on. It gets down and dirty quickly.

When the first icy sphere struck Joe, he naturally figured someone was hidden in the haystacks having some fun at his expense. In fact, he shouted the name "Fred," believing that it was his cousin, Fred Irwin, up there.

After looking closely around the barn, Joe found that he was alone. After visiting Fred's house later, he was assured that the snowball-slinging culprit was not his cousin.

Upon his return to the barn, Joe was again pelted by a snowball, and then another. Somehow, word got out in the sparsely populated area that something was awry in the barn down at Wilson's place.

There certainly was. In Joe's subsequent entry into the barn, he was hit or missed by a flurry of snowballs. From high above, as if out of nowhere, they came. From the left, from the right they came.

Curious neighbors vouched for the young man as they witnessed the phenomenon and eventually dared to enter the barn.

They, too, were victimized by the invisible thrower. Through the day and into the night the snowballs streamed. All were certain these were not the droppings of dripping or melting ice–they seemed to be formed by phantom fingers and tossed willy-nilly inside the big bank barn.

According to a later story in the *Honey Brook Herald*, the growing crowd of young men tried all they could to solve and resolve the matter.

At one point, they formulated a strategy. "The plan," the newspaper reported, had been to do picket duty around the barn until the supposed intruder was caught."

However, frigid weather forced the men to cancel that plan. Throughout the episode, thorough searches of the barn–in and out of every haystack, stall, and storage area–were made, and the building was repeatedly deemed devoid of any human inhabitants.

Then, very strange things started to happen.

Fred Irwin did eventually join his cousin and the others. At one point, he became the center of attention.

"During the search," the *Herald* article continued, "someone called attention to the words, 'TAKE CARE,' on the back of Fred Irwin's coat, seemingly written there with a piece of chalk.

"This was erased, and Fred and another lad ascended to the overhead, one on each side, with instructions to watch from that point of vantage for any other unusual manifestations. In less than two minutes on turning around to each other, both had writing on the backs of their coats."

Eventually, Absolom Wilson became quite unnerved by the events taking place in his barn. At one point, he attempted a kind of exorcism.

"He brought a big, hard snowball into the house," the newspaper writer noted, "and stuck in into a pot of boiling water with the remark, 'I'm going to kill that devil of a witch,' whose work he firmly believed it to be.

While hoping to rid his barn of the "devil of a witch," Wilson also wanted to rid his property of the strangers who descended upon it to witness the snowball-throwing ghost (or witch).

He had work to do. It was private property. And, whether what happened was the work of a pitching poltergeist or an elaborate hoax, Wilson was determined to downplay the entire matter and downsize the crowds.

As the newspaper concluded, "Affairs finally reached such a pass that as a matter of self protection from the additional annoyance of inquisitive visitors the impression was allowed to prevail that it had been the work of a slight of hand performer."

But, Absolom Wilson...and Fred Irwin...and Joe Morrison...knew better.

In fact, in 1913, an aging Fred Irwin surfaced at a Downingtown notary's office.

His son brought him there to make a detailed affirmation of the episode "in order to preserve an account of the mysterious transactions in a manner not to be gainsaid by some future historian."

📖

The Bell Tower, Eastern College

SUZY, THE GHOST OF EASTERN COLLEGE

Two very fine and very beautiful college campuses stand virtually shoulder-to-shoulder in the Radnor/St. Davids section of extreme northern Delaware County.

Both are rooted in religious traditions, both were founded in the mid-1950s, both are set on former "Main Line" estates...and both are haunted.

Established in 1957 by the Missionary Sisters of the Sacred Heart of Jesus, Cabrini College spreads across

54

112 acres, while nearby Eastern College encompasses some 100 beautifully-landscaped acres.

As we will visit Eastern College's haunted halls of higher learning first, a clarification about its beginnings.

It was technically founded in 1932 as a department of the Eastern Baptist Theological Seminary. The college became a separate entity in 1952 when it opened on the grounds of the former estate of leather and lumber magnate Charles Spittall Walton Sr.

When the college moved to that beautiful location, it inherited one of the most magnificent residences in all of Philadelphia's western suburbs.

Set on a rise above Willow Lake, "Walmarthon" included 55 rooms within its 18-inch thick walls and under its eleven gables.

So dubbed by combining the name of his wife, Martha, with his own surname, Walton's mansion was designed by D. Knickerbacker Boyd in the styles of a Spanish Mission and Italian villa. Its most noteworthy exterior feature was an eight-sided bell tower. Its interior was appointed with a blend of classic appointments such as leaded glass, Mercer tiles, and intricately carved oak woodwork and the very latest of creature comforts.

Charles S. Walton Sr. died at the age of 54 in 1916, and his widow continued to live there until her death in 1932. The seminary purchased the mansion, several outbuildings, and 41 surrounding acres in 1951 and opened the college a year later.

Following several reconfigurations and adaptations, Walmarthon became Walton Hall, the student center of Eastern College.

Sometime around 1961, the municipal Fire Marshal inspected the building and ordered that its third floor be closed to public access for safety reasons.

And, according to college archivist, retired history professor and long-time faculty secretary Dr. Frederick J. Boehlke, it was about that time the ghostly activity in Walton Hall started to be noticed.

It is worth noting that the floors of Walton Hall are numbered in the European style. Thus, one enters on the ground floor. The next story is the "first floor," etc. Thus, the "third floor" of the building is actually the fourth level. That all plays a role in some of the reports of the hauntings of Walton Hall.

Dr. Boehlke, a scholarly historian who nonetheless seems intrigued by the ghost stories of Walton Hall, believes that when the third floor was ordered sealed and abandoned by the Fire Marshal, a mysterious breeding ground for a haunting was created.

When contacted for his thoughts about the matter, Dr. Boehlke said he could recall no mention of the stories before 1961. The genial archivist promised to look into the matter, search the archives, and share what information, if any, he might find.

What he found was a file folder that held within it whatever had been saved regarding the ghost of Walton Hall.

Slim as it may have been, the file did contain one important and impressive document written in 1977 by student Bruce Miller for his American Folklore class.

As Miller stated in the closing line of his research paper, "It is my hope that this paper will be used by successive researchers in an attempt to broaden our understanding."

Your hope, Mr. Miller, has been fulfilled.

As it was a paper submitted for a college class, Miller's "A Study of Suzy Walton, Legend and Fact" drew on classic folkloric sources. He slotted the stories told at Eastern College into motifs and classifications accepted by folklorists.

WALTON HALL, ADMINISTRATION BUILDING.
EASTERN BAPTIST COLLEGE, ST. DAVIDS, PA.

Walmarthon

Miller also mentioned a story written in a previously published ghost story book, but found that account rife with inaccuracies and misinterpretations.

What he did find were wildly divergent tales told by several people at the college that all led to one assumption–Walton Hall is haunted.

Just who haunts the old Walmarthon mansion, and perhaps other sites on the Eastern campus, did and still does remain uncertain.

The ghost is generally believed to be that of little Suzy Walton, the granddaughter of Charles S. Walton Sr.

Suzanne Walton was born in 1923 and succumbed to the ravages of lupus in 1929. As matters of fact, Suzy was not born at Walmarthon, did not die there, and probably spent little time there.

Still, several legends have grown around her all-too-brief life, and all point toward her being the ghost that is said to haunt the third floor/fourth level/bell tower of Walton Hall.

In his research, Miller spoke with the secretary to the Dean of Students who had heard that little Suzy either fell or was pushed from a fourth-floor balcony and plummeted to her death.

Another college employee, the Director of Alumni, recalled hearing that Suzy was murdered on that third floor, raped and suffocated at the age of about 19.

Yet another source told Miller she believed Suzy hanged herself from a beam in the bell tower.

These stories, as Miller and family fact confirmed, are simply not true.

But what of the ghostly occurrences in that bell tower, on that third floor, and around the campus?

There is the very real possibility that the ghost, "whether it exists or not," as Miller put it, is not that of Suzy Walton.

While Dr. Boehlke suggested that the stories still told by students and teachers "seem to be imagined," he did not totally dismiss them.

In a random sampling of students asked about the ghost stories on their campus, it became clear that many, if not most, have heard about them. Two members of the class of 2002, both of whom preferred that their names not be used, offered their first-person encounters with the ghost they still call "Suzy."

"All I can tell you," said one coed, "is that I have often felt as if someone about waist-high was walking next to me over at Walton. It's not easy to describe the feeling, and it's not what I would think to be a classical 'ghost,' but I have just felt that someone was there, with me. I felt as if it was a little girl, and that she was trying to get my attention. Sometimes, I even caught myself looking over and down, as if I might catch a glimpse of her."

When asked what version of the story of the death of Suzy Walton she had heard, she was surprisingly on the mark. "Oh, I think she died when she was about six or seven of some disease," she said.

Another female student had heard the more graphic story of Suzy being shoved by a servant from the third-floor balcony.

"I heard she was a little girl who was murdered," she said. "And, I know that one time I was walking down from Walton Hall to the library when I swear a little girl ran right in front of me. She just dashed across my path, coming from out of nowhere and disappearing in a flash. Was that the ghost? I don't know, but it scared the heck out of me. I know that other students have claimed to see the little girl in their rooms and other buildings on campus. Yeah, I think there's a ghost here, and that's OK with me, as long as it keeps its distance!"

Up in that closed-off third floor, used only for storage, several teachers and students say they have heard the shuffling of feet, a pathetic whimpering sound, and the occasional echo of a sobbing child.

Another phantom, that of a middle-aged man, has been seen walking along the edge of Willow Lake between Walmarthon and the Gate House.

That ghost, of course, could well be Mr. Walton himself, just keeping watch over his beloved old Walmarthon.

Seven Stars Inn

THE SECRETS OF SEVEN STARS

While traffic these days zooms through the intersection of Route 23 and Hoffecker Road in East Vincent Township, there was a time when the pace was considerably slower and the temptation was great to stop for refreshment at a wayside inn there.

Today, that old inn is a destination for many people who seek its elegant atmosphere and fine food. Today, it is the Seven Stars Inn.

Today, it holds within its ancient walls many secrets, mysteries, and a ghost or two.

Built near a Lenni-Lenape village in about 1720, the building started as the home of Gerhard Brumbach, a miller and farmer.

According to a history commissioned by the owners of the Seven Stars Inn, it was in May, 1736, when Brumbach petitioned the court of the King to establish a tavern along the Ridge Road, now Route 23.

The area was undergoing an 18th century version of suburban sprawl, with settlers pouring in and traffic plodding by Brumbach's property.

On the ground that he was frequently oppressed by travelers whom he was obliged to entertain, and that there were no publick houses within twenty miles below nor thirty miles above his place on the Great Road which leads from Philadelphia to the Iron Works, and from thence to Conestoga....

...Brumbach was granted the license.

Thus, well before the Colonies became States, the Seven Stars Inn (given that name by John Baker in 1804) has been a stopping-off point for travelers and diners.

The building has undergone much restoration and careful preservation. An ancient well and other architectural peculiarities have been discovered, and many other mysteries remain unresolved there.

One is the name. Even the most intense historical research cannot definitively determine its origin. In its official history, it is stated that "Seven Stars" might have come from a long-gone seven-way intersection there, or the seven stars of the Big Dipper, or the seven years of the American Revolution, or a throwback to British pubs of the same name.

But, far more intense mysteries prevail there. Such as, who murdered Rachel Parker in the old stables sometime in the late 1780s? And, what function did a 30-feet long subterranean passageway serve? It was another buried secret found by restorers in the 1970s.

For the mystery that vaulted the Seven Stars Inn to the pages of this book, we turned to Aloma Fisher, who has been a member of the inn's custodial staff for nearly three decades.

"She's the historian here," proprietor Frank Cacciutti affirmed. Aloma, he assured us, knew all the stories and lore.

Indeed she did. She reeled off anecdotes with alacrity as we sat in the inn talking of history and mystery.

One of those anecdotes stands out as one Aloma will never forget, and perhaps never fully understand.

"It was late morning one day," she began. "I was upstairs in the dining room on the second floor. There was lots of noise outside–jackhammers going, you know–they were fixing the road.

"I turned around and at the top of the steps there was a figure. It was a young person, with a white blouse on, puffy sleeves–you know how they used to wear them.

"The figure was also wearing riding pants or something like that. It was a young person. And honestly, I don't know if it was a female or a male, because the hair was pulled back."

Aloma *did* know that she was the only living being up there at the time. And within seconds of it appearing, the figure disappeared.

Who could it have been? Why did it appear to her?

She harkened to the time that Benjamin Brownback was the innkeeper there. He passed away in 1786, and it was his 85-year old widow, Rachel, who was murdered there.

"She was killed in the stables and they never found out who killed her," Aloma continued. "It could be related to that. After all, she was killed in the riding stables, and this figure seemed to be wearing a riding outfit."

Aloma said she was not frightened by the sudden appearance. In fact, her reaction was somewhat novel.

"I turned around and it looked at me and vanished and I said, 'Well, come back here!'. But it didn't," she laughed.

Aloma believes the spirit may have been stirred into manifesting itself because of the roadwork being done on Route 23 outside. Perhaps, she believes, it was shaken out of its dormancy to protest the commotion.

That brief encounter was Aloma's only sighting of that secret specter of Seven Stars. But, a chance "reading" of the inn a bit later added more mystery to the mix.

A well-known medium happened to drop by for dinner one evening and offered an unsolicited assessment of the otherworldly activity there.

"She felt the presence of a man lying on the floor in one of the back bedrooms," Aloma recalled.

That bedroom is now a dining room, and it could well be the resting-place for a ghost, according to a tale that has circulated amongst the restaurant employees.

"One of the former owners," Aloma said, "was a workaholic, and he died at the foot of the steps on the main floor. He literally worked himself to death!"

Aloma admitted there was nothing much more to the story. "It's a hearsay story," she said. But, it may have served as a baseline for that second secret of Seven Stars.

Aloma Fisher was quick to affirm that she is intrigued by all of this.

"I do believe in ghosts," she said, without hesitation.

In fact, she has been touched–perhaps literally–by the spirit world in her own home in Spring City.

"When I first moved in there," she said, "the place was a wreck. We had lots to fix up and clean up.

"I was standing there and I felt a nudge. I almost fell into my dryer! I turned around and couldn't see anybody. I said 'Now look, I'm trying to fix your house up! Just leave me alone!'"

That seemed to quell the ghostly goings-on and calm Aloma's nerves. It wasn't soon, though, until the unseen entity made its presence known once more.

"I was sitting on the bed one time and I actually moved over because someone sat on the bed next to me," Aloma said.

She could actually feel the bed sag and saw a depression in the sheets, as if some invisible "bottom" had plopped itself down with her.

And that, Aloma said, has happened several more times.

She feels the spirit may be that of a woman who lived (and died) in the house that makes up the other side of her semi-detached residence. If it really is that woman's ghost, it might have taken on a voyeuristic tendency during yet another manifestation.

"When my husband was still alive," Aloma said. "We never closed the bathroom door when we were in there. One time he came up to me and told me he thought our ghost was back. I asked him why. He told me he thought someone was staring at him while he was going to the bathroom!"

Aloma chuckled when she told that story. But she would very much like to learn more about the spirit of her own home and the secrets of the Seven Stars Inn.

In both cases, she readily accepts the mysteries. As for the Seven Stars, she said she is "very much at home there."

Apparently, the resident spirits of the old inn are quite at home there, as well. And Aloma Fisher would very much like to learn who they might be and what they might be seeking.

The Scarlett House

THE HOUSE ON HESSIAN HILL

Described as "a gracious charmer of another era," and "an authentic four square American Victorian," the Scarlett House Bed and Breakfast in Kennett Square is all of that, and more.

Well insulated from busy W. State State Street, the opulent granite home was built by the influential Scarlett family in 1910.

As a bed and breakfast, it is ideally situated at the edge of town and beautifully appointed with every creature comfort a discriminating traveler would request or require.

Historically, it is positioned on Hessian Hill, so named for the encampment of German mercenaries who aided British Generals Howe and Cornwallis in their (successful) campaign against the Colonials at the Battle of Brandywine in 1777.

That bit of lore may also serve as the source of another quality of the Scarlett House–a quality that has emerged to certain guests who have enjoyed enjoyable–if not uneventful–stays there.

In November, 2000, Christina Powell became the innkeeper at the Scarlett House. While she has not had any experiences there and remains quite skeptical about the notion of ghosts, she did confirm that it didn't take long for her to be introduced to the very real possibility that the Scarlett House has an eternal guest or two.

"The first night I moved in here," she said. "They said something about it. I was exhausted. I though to myself, 'Don't show up tonight, I'm just way too tired for that!"

They were Sam and Jane Snyder, the previous innkeepers. *That* was the collective body of speculative evidence that the beautiful mansion was, well, haunted.

The Snyders had owned and operated the B&B since 1994. For 30 years or so, they had traveled in more than 70 countries and stayed mostly in bed and breakfasts, and when their Long Island nest emptied, they decided they'd give it a go at operating their own B&B.

After a three-year, 100-property search, they found the Scarlett House. Sam Snyder was a cook in the army and still loved to cook. He and Jane also loved to meet new people. So, when Sam retired from a successful career as an interior designer, he and Jane settled into the innkeepers' life in Kennett Square.

For two years, Sam put the B&B together while Jane worked out the last years of her teaching career. Upon her retirement, she joined her husband.

It wasn't long until the affable couple was introduced to their "permanent" guests.

66

"My first encounter was with a Chinese lady who was living in California," Sam said. "She proceeded to tell me that there was a ghost in her room. She just volunteered that. She just came over and asked if I knew that there was a ghost in the house."

Sam admitted that he was a bit taken by surprise, unprepared for the revelation.

"Actually," he continued, "the woman said the ghost was in one room, and she didn't feel threatened by it."

The visitor's observation stirred Sam's curiosity. He knew what the land had been used for during the Revolution, and added that ingredient into food for thought. Together with his wife, a retired history teacher, they blended a stew of speculation.

"Jane and I thought about what she said and we wondered if what she saw or felt might be one of the Hessians," Sam said.

And, Jane wondered if anyone in the Scarlett family had died in the house.

"Later," she confirmed, "we met William Scarlett, who was in his 90s at the time, and he told us the only funeral he could remember in the house happened during the first World War, and it wasn't someone who had died in the house."

The Scarlett elder did note that a member of his family did pass away in the house, but he was middle-aged, and did not die in the room where the guest detected the ghost.

That room? A room the Snyders dubbed the "Victorian Rose Room."

Awhile after that first unexpected report, another guest offered a *déjà vu* declaration.

"A woman simply asked if we knew that there was a ghost in the room," Sam said.

He said he didn't respond right away, opting instead to hee-haw around until she spoke.

"What she told me," Sam continued, "was just what the first lady had told us. Except that she felt the entity hovering over the bed. She could almost see its imprint on the ceiling. And then, she said that she looked at the clock and the time was spinning around!"

The woman didn't wake her husband, who was sleeping next to her. She said she watched the phenomena with amazement, and was never threatened or unnerved by what was happening.

And, what happened that night happened in the Victorian high backed walnut bed in...the Victorian Rose Room.

The plot thickened in short order when not one, but four guests related their collective tales.

"They said they were playing cards in the 'Ladies' Parlor' when they felt a presence pass through them," Jane said.

Still another off-handed comment came from another woman who had stayed in the Victorian Rose Room.

But, this comment came with an interesting addendum. She said the ghost was that of a young male, perhaps around 13 years old.

"She gave the ghost a name," Jane said. "She called him 'Frederick.' She just said she felt he was a 'Frederick.'"

Or, could it have been a "Friedrich?" Could it have been the ghost of, perhaps, a drummer boy, courier, or bugler from the ranks of the Hessians who once occupied the hillside?

The Snyders' strong feelings for history and sentiments for their resident ghost came to the fore.

"That woman told us she felt the ghost of 'Frederick' in the Victorian Rose Room, and that when she went to the other side of the house she felt a spirit there, too."

68

So, Sam and Jane decided to try to meet their presumed Hessian houseguest head-on.

"We hunted for this ghost the whole time we were in there," Jane said.

Her husband added, almost embarrassingly, "We actually slept in the Victorian Rose Room, hoping to have an experience!"

Did they have that experience? Alas, no. The closest they came was on one dark and stormy (but otherwise uneventful) night. "The one night there was a loud thunderstorm," Jane chuckled, "but Sam slept right through it."

"I would love to see a ghost," Jane said.

Sam added, "And we don't know how many other guests have had those feelings. It was interesting that when one of the ladies came down and asked if we had a ghost, we didn't know what to say.

"We didn't know whether it was a plus or a minus, something bad or good." *(Read the Foreword of this book, Sam).*

He did point out that at least one of the women who had an experience with 'Frederick' did come back, and did request the Victorian Rose Room.

And although the Snyders did not promote the ghostly side of the Scarlett House, they would readily discuss it with anyone who asked.

"We never made a big thing about it," Jane said. "When people came, we'd never tell them there was a ghost in the house."

Sam added, jokingly, "Only after they had checked out and we had their money!"

Christina Powell said she will probably retain the name of the Victorian Rose Room, but may change the names of other chambers to reflect her botanical training and background.

As for the ghosts, she has adopted the Snyders' philosophy. "It's not that I disbelieve," the current keeper of the Scarlett House said, "I just don't think about it."

But both the Snyders and Ms. Powell seem to agree that a benign ghost or two at an historic bed and breakfast can't be all bad. *(Read the Foreword of this book, Christina).*

The Scarlett House

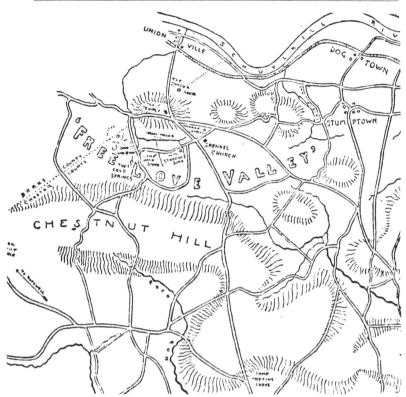

FREE LOVE VALLEY,
THE BATTLE-AXES,
AND THE GHOST OF HANNAH SHINGLE

The title of this chapter opens many avenues for the imagination to explore.

What you are about to read may appear so wild, so implausible, so unreal that you may question that it did ever happen, or could ever happen.

What's more, you may question that it could ever have happened in such an unlikely setting as a tranquil valley in extreme northern Chester County.

71

Yet, it was there where naked men, women, and children once romped; where a cult known as "Battle-Axes" once worshiped, and where the ghost of a murdered woman wanders.

Heady stuff for North Coventry Township, quiet then and quiet now.

Let us turn time back to 1841 and examine what the renowned historian W. Edmunds Claussen called "one of the most bizarre societies ever to evolve out of the mind of man."

Let us also turn our maps to the page where a long valley spreads out below Chestnut Hill and a series of knolls between the Schuylkill River and French Creek.

It is Free Love Valley. And how it got that name is almost beyond belief.

A precious piece of regional history is a 1930 book, *Theophilus: The Battle-Axe*, by Charles Coleman Sellers.

Its 67 pages are packed with intrigue, scandal, and tales that boggle even the most open of modern minds.

Sellers began with a description of the swath of Chester County countryside known as "Free Love Valley."

The name is not upon the maps, and rarely heard, even among the people of the valley themselves, who can permit it a certain jocular currency, now that the old days of fear and hatred, and blind, wild exultation have gone by, and there linger only shadowy memories, stories of a strange religion that is a laughing matter now, as often as not, of its peculiar rites, of mysterious deaths, and haunted burials.

The "Theophilus" of Sellers' title was Theophilus Ransom Gates, a shadowy figure who came to Pennsylvania from Connecticut and founded a strange cult he called the "Battle-Axes."

Gates employed a distorted interpretation of a disturbing passage from the Old Testament (Jeremiah) for the name of his intended flock. He instructed his

72

followers to rise up against religious persecution and governmental intrusion.

Those "Battle-Axes," or "Gatesites," as they were sometimes known, survived for only a few years, and their legacy is faint in Chester County lore, but from their time and that place have spun many tales of murder, mystery, and ghosts.

The epicenter of it all is Shenkel Church, from which Free Love Valley extended westward to and just over the Berks County line.

Several landmarks, some more obscure than others, remain from the days of the Battle-Axes and Free Love Valley.

At Cold Springs, members of the cult gathered, naked, to cleanse themselves of worldly corruption.

Several homes or ruins were once inhabited by Gates' followers–and foes.

And the stately Shenkel UCC is itself very much a part of the weird cult and its aftermath.

Even the pastor at the church at the time of this writing alluded to the underside of the history of the lovely sanctuary. He could only imagine his predecessor's reaction when a group of cult members traipsed, one-by-one, down the aisle of the church wearing nothing but their "birthday suits."

That scene actually did play out at Shenkel, as the Battle-Axes rose in defiance against the preaching of Rev. John Guldin at the then-Reformed church. Rev. Guldin was one of several area pastors who condemned the cult and paid varying emotional and professional prices for doing so.

As Sellers wrote, "The whole little mob of them would gather at one house, clothing and morals abandoned in the ecstasies of being perfect. There are stories that the whole crew was to be seen at times, prancing, crying to the sky, bare bodies glistening in the sun, arms trembling rigidly in air, all in full view of Shenkel Church."

Mind you, readers, this was the 1840s, not the 1960s.

The "prophet" Gates died in 1846, and by about 1857, the cult had run its course. Its members aging, arrested, or uninterested, the Battle-Axes, Sellers wrote, "sank rapidly into the semi-oblivion of scattered legend and hushed scandal."

The titillating tales of Gates' followers aside, the valley that stretches beyond Shenkel Church and the knoll of the same name holds within it one of the best-known ghost stories in all of Pennsylvania.

The tale was given impetus by artist and writer Patrick Reynolds in his popular *Pennsylvania Profiles* newspaper and book feature. Under the heading of "Questionably Dead Citizens," Reynolds encapsulated the story of the heinous murder and ghostly reappearance of Hannah Shingle.

Hannah's story has been handed down through several generations and was repeated by Sellers, Claussen, and other chroniclers of life and lore in that part of Chester County.

Sellers framed a part of the story within the bounds of the Shenkel Church graveyard.

"The neat little graveyard was a haunted place, if one can believe it now," he wrote. "Two murdered women are buried there, and two men died unnatural deaths close by, not to mention the despondent boatman who hanged himself on a great chestnut tree on Catfish Lane, just over the hill."

Now dotted with sumptuous modern homes, the hillocks and glens of the area were once wrapped by less-than-desirable conditions.

Canallers and cattlemen, miners and foundry workers were not the most civil of citizens, and they all prowled the area in the mid to late 1800s.

Nearby iron furnaces spewed their fiery cinders into the sky. Down by Warwick Furnace, the cluster of homes where workers dwelled was called "Hell's Hinges."

It was, by all accounts, a wild and often lawless place.

There lived in that valley a 61-year old woman named Hannah Shingle. Folks said that in her youth, she was beautiful and much sought-after by local beaus. But time had not been good to her. Physical and emotional ravages had turned her into a crone her neighbors would, with charity, describe as "eccentric."

Amid thick underbrush and crumbling walls, Hannah maintained a small, unkempt farm just down from Shenkel Knoll, in view of the church. Known in local legend as Hannah *Shingle*, she was a direct descendant of Henry *Shenkel*, from whose family she inherited the farm. Interestingly, her tombstone in the church graveyard seems to read Hannah *Shengle*. The name has also been recorded in some documents as *Shingel*. But, I stray from the story.

Some said Hannah had stashed a good amount of gold somewhere on her property. Most dismissed that as poppycock.

Although she had several relatives in the area, Hannah opted to dwell in her old age alone and was visited only by youthful tormenters she would chase from her farm with gun or hatchet in hand.

It was October 21, 1855 when one of the few individuals who was trusted by Hannah Shingle came to check on her. John Miller, hired by Hannah to do odd jobs around her property from time to time, knocked on the front door of her little hermitage, but there was no answer. He knew at that moment that something was awry.

He summoned a couple of neighbors to join him in a search for the old woman. He feared the worst.

Together, several local men burst through the locked front door. They found a stew simmering on the stove, flames flickering in the fireplace, and an eerie silence. Quietly and cautiously, they made their way up the narrow staircase.

John Miller's fear was substantiated when, to the horror of all, the bloody, bludgeoned body of Hannah Shingle was discovered on the bed of her tiny upstairs bedroom.

Hannah's head had been crushed and nearly severed. Blood dripped into pools on the floor and splattered the walls. It was a grisly sight that repelled even the strongest man in the search party.

There was evidence that an intruder had used a ladder to gain access to Hannah's room. Further, it appeared that the old woman might have put up a fight by grabbing the hatchet she kept under her bed for protection. In tragic irony, that very hatchet was the murder weapon.

What's more, there appeared to be a man's footprint, cast in blood, on one of the woman's pillows.

Hysteria spread in a wave across the valley and beyond. The local newspapers bristled with lurid headlines and graphic accounts of the murder. Ghoulish sightseers came to see the house where Hannah was brutally murdered. Even years later, it was noted that a piece of ragged furniture from Hannah's humble home drew a wildly inflated price at resale because it bore crimson stains from Hannah's blood.

John Miller was detained, questioned, and released by the local authorities. Some former "Battle-Axes" were hauled in and interrogated. The constable, Billy Rader, even sought the advice of a medium. It is said the psychic investigator may have provided a detailed and damning description of the killer, but no such information would ever be admitted in court, so it was dismissed.

The fact that the murder took place in a remote section of northern Chester County did not deter District Attorney J. Smith Futhy (later President Judge of Chester County Courts) from mounting a vigorous investigation. Despite his and the constable's best efforts, Hannah's murderer was never found.

There were some bizarre twists and turns as the investigation proceeded. One man reportedly hanged himself (from a stout tree at what is now the corner of Valley View Road and Catfish Lane) after he was fingered as the possible culprit. Some believed his suicide was his confession.

Another chief suspect at the time was a worker at the Schuylkill Canal yard in Unionville. He was found in possession of blood-saturated coveralls, but in those crude, pre-DNA days, even that evidence was not enough to have him arrested.

It is difficult to sort out fact from legend from those days, but it was reported that on his deathbed, the boatyard worker did confess to the murder . However, that has never been documented.

From nearly the moment Hannah Shingle's body was lowered into its grave, stories of her ghost began to circulate in the valley.

Her spirit seemed to wander between her simple grave at Shenkel Church and her old home not far away.

In September, 1879, the *Daily Pottstown Ledger* carried the account of a man named Montgomery Campbell, who told a reporter that a pale, headless spirit had approached him as he rode past Hannah's old springhouse.

Campbell was startled, but had the presence of mind to stop and attempt to communicate with the ghost. The more he questioned it, the fainter it became, until it faded into the night.

In the article, Campbell stated: "Having seen that spook with my own eyes, I am convinced there is such a thing, and no matter what others say, I am going to stick to that opinion."

Rev. Brian C. Hardee, pastor of Shenkel Church who resides in the parsonage just below Hannah's grave, said he often sees folks gathering by the tombstone. He's not sure if they are maintaining a vigil for her ghost or simply paying their respects.

And, current residents of the property where the murder took place say they have had no ghostly encounters there. Hannah's old house has long-since tumbled into ruin, and only faint foundations remain, they said. But, are they correct in that assessment?

There are those who believe whole-heartedly that Hannah Shingle's restless, forlorn, and sometimes headless ghost rambles in the brambles around her old homestead. Some believe psychic readings of energies in the old Shingle property have revealed a strong, benign presence there.

While much of the factual material and documentation regarding Hannah's murder has been lost in time, psychic research has suggested that the murder did take place inside the farmhouse that still stands on the unfortunate woman's old homestead. The springhouse on the property, an energy reading detected, was also a site of orgiastic rituals–likely those of the Battle-Axe cult.

One resident of the area, who declined to give her name, said she had an odd experience while cycling past Hannah's place.

"There's not much to it," she said, "but as I was going over the little bridge over the stream near what was her house, I could swear I saw the fleeting glimpse of an old woman glide across the road and up into the weeds. It was colorless, if you know what I mean, and seemed to glance over at me for a second or two as it passed. I know that some people say the ghost, if there is one, is headless, but this, uh, this thing, certainly had a head, and it looked right at me!

"That's really all I can say. I had heard the stories of the murder and the ghost and all, and maybe I was just imagining things, but I never saw anything like it before, and never have since."

When asked if she thought she had seen the ghost of Hannah Shingle, the young woman thought long and replied, "Well, part of me says there can be no such things as ghosts, but another part of me would like to believe there are. I guess that given where I was, what happened there, and what I saw, I might have seen her ghost. But, who knows?"

The grave of Hannah Shingle at Shenkel Church

The Red Rose Inn

GHOSTS AND ROSES

Set on each lace-covered table in the beautiful dining rooms of the Red Rose Inn is a vase with one red
rose.

Just up the Baltimore Pike from the restaurant is
the memorial rose garden of the Conard-Pyle Company, grower of Star Roses.

It is a cheery, colorful place in the busy crossroads
village of Jennersville, this Red Rose Inn.

Moreover, people have long said it is haunted.

The modern course of U.S. Route 1 bypasses the
inn a couple hundred yards away, but the Red Rose
Inn continues to serve its clientele just as it did when
the Baltimore Pike was Colonial America's "main
street" and what is now Route 796 was a path used by
Delaware and Lenni-Lenape Indians.

It was in 1740 that a tavern was built at that intersection of commerce and cultures, and that tavern became the Red Rose.

The name can be traced to an ancient English custom of deeding property at the price of one red rose a year.

According to research done by David E. Conner at Lincoln University in 1980, the land upon which the tavern is situated was the site of one of only two such token payment arrangements in the colonies. It was arranged by the Penn family.

Although the inn did not become a licensed tavern for many years after its construction, it was certainly a trading post and way station for natives and settlers alike.

It was during those earliest years of the tavern when most of the ghost stories were rooted and in the oldest section of the building (additions were made in 1829 and 1968) that the most them play out.

The energies in the Red Rose Inn are so intense that they have drawn the attention of world-renowned psychics and mediums and writers of several books and newspapers.

For miles around, folks know–or think they know–of the ghosts of the inn.

One individual who responded to a call for ghost stories from this writer put the Red Rose at the top of her list.

She said she had heard several "they say" stories about a "haunted horseman" who trots eternally along the Baltimore Pike in front of the inn; of a young girl who hanged herself somewhere in the building; and of a ghostly Indian who has been seen and felt there.

Ghost-hunting parapsychologists have detected apparitions, and there is scarcely an employee at the Red Rose who has not had some sort of unexplained encounter–or knows someone who has.

As quaint and charming as the restaurant is, it is almost unbelievable that somewhere, on another plane within those walls, a crazy-quilt cast of ghostly characters goes about their business.

There is the Man in Plaid, perhaps the victim of a murder that took place in a field behind the inn. There is Indian Joe, and there is Emily.

The latter spirits are forever entwined in mystery, suspicion, and injustice.

As the story goes, a local native known by the white settlers as "Joe" was suspected of murdering the young daughter of an early innkeeper.

It was around the time of the French and Indian War, and being a native did not serve "Joe" well. Although evidence pointed away from him as the killer, he was convicted in a kangaroo court, hanged on the property, and buried in the dirt basement of the oldest part of the inn. After his lynching, the identity of the actual murderer was discovered. But, it was too late for "Joe."

His forlorn and sometimes cantankerous spirit still wanders through the inn, as does the innocent ghost of the little girl he was accused of murdering.

Her name is Emily.

With these legends and stories circulating through time, it is inevitable that the spirits of these individuals make themselves known from time to time.

Innkeeper Lee Covatta feels that if ghosts really do dwell in her lovely restaurant, they help to protect it. Sure, she has had odd things happen to her that could be attributable to ghosts, but she seems more inclined to attach real rather than surreal explanations to them.

The keeper of the folklore flame at the Red Rose is Lee's son and co-proprietor, Anthony Covatta.

It was, and forgive me here, a dark and stormy night when Tony went through a litany of adventures he has had in his 20-plus years at the Red Rose.

82

"Everything that happened to me transpired in the first couple of years I was here," Tony noted.

"I wasn't a believer at all," he added.

But, from almost the first day he spent working (and living) at the Red Rose, things started to happen.

One night he and a bartender were in an upstairs office and the dish washer was down in the kitchen, washing dishes.

As Tony and the bartender were reviewing procedures on how to close up at the end of the day, they were startled when a calculator on a table in back of them turned itself on, spun numbers as if unseen hands were working the keyboard, and reeled off paper from its roll.

The two men stood aghast, staring at the machine. To their shock, *another* calculator just over their shoulders clicked on and acted the very same way!

Tony and the bartender watched in amazement as the action went on for a few strange seconds.

They left the room and went downstairs. The visibly shaken bartender went home. Tony went into the kitchen where he was greeted by a visibly shaken dish washer.

As he approached the kitchen, Tony heard a loud bang and an odd whirring, crashing sound.

He stepped into the kitchen to discover that a double set of fans had flown from their setting, over the sinks, and onto the floor–still running.,

"The dish washer left," Tony said, "white as a sheet!"

His employees gone and his own nerves rattled, Tony then faced the unenviable task of going back upstairs to retire to the innkeeper's apartment, where he resided at the time.

The show was not yet over. The energy level was still quite intense.

"I heard all these doors slamming," he said. "Well, I thought the girl I was engaged to at the time was upstairs and she was mad about something and was slamming all the doors.

"It turned out that she was sitting on the couch, shaking like a leaf. Here, all the doors in the hallway–all four of them–were slamming. I asked her what was going on. She said that something just blew in through here like you wouldn't believe!"

That "something" was no breeze, no wind.

Another powerful event took place much later behind the bar, Tony recalled.

"One night I closed up the bar and went upstairs. I came down the next morning and a mirror on the wall behind the bar was smashed, face-down on the floor."

All the glass was broken, but was neatly crushed within the mirror frame.

"For that thing to fall like that," Tony said, "it would have had to slide down and take out three rows of liquor bottles that are stacked behind the bar. But, the bottles were untouched.

"All I can figure is that it flew straight out, about six feet, flipped over, and fell straight down!"

Tony Covatta is now a believer. He feels the Red Rose Inn is indeed haunted, and one more incident...one individual...thoroughly convinced him of that.

Emily.

"I had just gone into the master bedroom and was getting ready to go to bed," he said.

"I had just turned the TV on and my bedroom door opened up.

"There she was, standing at the top of the steps, looking down.

"It was a little girl, holding a doll, just like you'd see on TV or in any ghost story. Just a little girl standing there in what looked like an Easter dress. A stereotypical little ghost girl!"

"She just stood there for a few seconds...and vanished!"

Tony knew he was alone in the inn that night, and could only come to one conclusion–he had seen the ghost of Emily.

To his knowledge, no current employee or visitor to the inn has ever seen the ghost of "Indian Joe." But, the anonymous murdered man may have manifested himself more than once in the main dining room.

"He appears in the dining room from time to time," Tony said. Some of the waitresses have seen him. He's a guy in an ugly plaid jacket. They've looked over and seen a guy at, say, table A-2. Then, they went to get a pitcher of water to wait on him and he'd be gone!"

"Oh yeah, there are ghosts in here," Tony said. But as his mother noted, they are–with the exception of the strong poltergeistic slamming, crashing, and banging–harmless and innocent.

Even with its cast of ghostly characters, the Red Rose Inn remains as one of the Brandywine Valley's most quaint and respected restaurants and guest houses.

The boulders of French Creek at St. Peters Village

PHANTOMS OF FRENCH CREEK

Along Chester County's northwestern border with Berks County, French Creek seeps from its sources in the lakes of the state park that bears its name.

As it winds and wiggles its way to Phoenixville and its confluence with the Schuylkill River, it squeezes through the powerful granite boulders in a deep ravine known as the Falls of French Creek.

86

It is a storied land, steeped in mystery and legend. It is where rumors of silver and gold deposits sent fools on prospecting missions. It is where thieves and ne'er-do-wells connived and cavorted. It is where miners and quarrymen ravaged the landscape.

It is also a place where wraiths ramble among the rocks and phantoms stalk the falls.

High over those falls is St. Peters Village, a charming collection of ca. 1880 buildings dominated by the St. Peter's Inn.

Built in 1881 by Davis Knauer as a summer resort adjacent to his black granite quarry, the inn became a cool haven for 19th century tourists brought in on the trains of the French Creek Branch of the Wilmington & Northern Railroad.

Is that ornate, Victorian hotel that positively *looks haunted*...haunted?

If the experiences of workers there over the years are to be believed...yes!

Many have told the tales of the crying baby, the strolling lady, and the gentle old man.

They are the ghosts of St. Peter's Inn.

Patty Powell, co-owner and manager of the inn, said, "We've had several incidents that people talk about.

"Lights come on when nobody has turned them on–that's happened a lot downstairs. And, we've heard doors slam shut on floors where there was nobody."

A woman who worked at the inn had heard stories that a forlorn woman had committed suicide on the second floor several years ago. She is convinced the woman she has seen in the corner of her eye from time to time in the main dining room is that woman's ghost.

She declined to give her name, but told us that she had often caught the fleeting glimpse of what she could best describe as a young and well-proportioned woman standing at a window, looking over the falls. When her eyes made contact with the shadowy form, it vanished.

The crying baby is a phenomenon reported as early as the 1940s in the hotel. Employees closing for the night, transients staying in upstairs rooms and various other folks reported hearing the echoing sound of a baby crying somewhere–they could never determine exactly where–in the big building. No source of the baby's haunting has ever been offered.

The St. Peter's Inn

And then, there's Herbie. That's the name given to a ghostly presence reported in recent years. In *a Daily Local News* article in 1996, writer Jan Riemer reported on an employee and a former owner of the inn who both had encounters with the kind and gentle ghost they believed was that of a deceased village baker named Herb Hinkle.

Herb lived in the inn, they said, and was known as a generous man who would slip a free cookie to a child and go out of his way to be nice to people.

Even the most gracious of ghosts can still scare the bejeebers out of a mere mortal.

Such was the case for several workers who continuously heard footsteps, watched as doors opened, closed, or locked themselves and felt as if someone was looking over their shoulders. After a while, these events and emotions were blamed on "Herbie."

St. Peter's Village, and that entire little valley of the French Creek including Knauertown, Warwick, and Coventryville has had more than its share of ghostly goings-on.

Under the headline of "SPOOK, OR WHAT?" a front-page article in the February 22, 1882 *Reading Eagle* featured a dispatch from "Y.R.," in St. Peter's.

The correspondent told readers that "scarlet fever has been bad throughout the area," that "the temperance excitement was dying down," and that the neighborhood was engaged in "catching muskrats and getting ready for spring work."

But the big story was The Spook!

"This usually quiet neighborhood," Y.R. wrote, "is now convulsed with excitement caused by a supernatural wonder commonly called a 'spook.'

"Old men and women, middle-aged and young are talking about the 'ghost' with bated breath and fear."

The correspondent noted that the hysteria had rekindled tales of Hannah Shingle's murder and "water smelling, fortune telling, spiritualism, and the spook of May's old graveyard." It was all quite startling, the writer assured the reader.

The reports of the ghost came from several people in several places, all centered along the upper French Creek.

"It is asserted that one of the dashing young beaux of this neighborhood saw the spook last Thursday night and now declares that he will not go out again at night, until the moon is full."

Another man saw the ghost walking ahead of him as he crossed French Creek on what was described as "Samuel Lightfoot's farm."

This time, that witness swore, the ghost sang!

"It turned into a swampy place," the account continued, "and sang in a hollow voice, the following:

How far from heaven?
How far from hell?
Hold here! Where is my gold?
Buried! Buried! Buried!!"

Apparently, Y.R. faced the same dilemma modern collectors of ghost stories face when then trade a teller's story for anonymity. "I would give you the man's name," Y.R. stated, "but he told what he had seen under the injunction of secrecy."

The singing spirit's reference to buried gold ignited old memories of buried treasure or veins of precious metals in the area. Folks gathered around in stores and barnyards to discuss the old stories of the "old days" and the more recent tales of the neighborhood "spook."

That "spook" (it should be noted that in that area and at that time, the common description of a ghost was "spook," or to the Pennsylvania Germans, "schpuk") was described as moving swiftly, possessive of long gray hair and beard, and a "shrill and hollow voice."

"It makes me creep to hear the neighbors describe it," Y.R. admitted.

Just who was this ghost? The writer offered a possible answer.

"An old colored woman by the name of Williams used to say that a peddler was murdered on the

Pughtown Road, and his body buried without shroud or coffin, and that the spook now prowling around the neighborhood is that of the murdered peddler."

There is another dusty story from the Falls of French Creek in which the central character *rose from the dead* in a most unusual fashion.

It was the middle of the 19th century when a band of horse thieves and counterfeiters sought and found refuge among the caverns and boulders below St. Peter's Village.

Once more, the details of the story are sorely lacking, but the tale was handed down generation to generation, and is likely rooted in truth.

The outlaws, who had stolen horses in Chester, Berks, Lancaster, Montgomery, and Philadelphia counties, discovered that they could hideout easily in the creek-creased boulder field. There was no hotel there at the time, few buildings, few people, and no law.

But, constables, cops, and sheriffs from other jurisdictions drew a bead on the bandits and word got out that their rocky lair was about to be raided.

The leader of the pack was said to have made a rather ingenious escape. He somehow arranged for everything to fall in place and summoned a doctor, a minister, an undertaker, and gravediggers to fake his death and burial.

Perhaps paying them in his bogus bills, the chap managed to pull it off. He could certainly not be arrested if he was buried six feet under. What's more, by the time, if ever, the authorities got wise to his ruse, he'd be long gone and far away.

As it turned out, the lawmen did get wise. The fugitive slipped up and somebody down St. Peter's way tipped off the police that they might want to check the culprit's coffin in his grave at a nearby church cemetery.

They did, and they found a 150-pound bag of sand instead of a dead horse thief.

It was soon discovered that the crook had made his escape to Miami County, Ohio, where he did, in fact, undeniably, positively, die a few years later.

PRISSY...AND THE SKELETONS
OF THE BLUE BALL TAVERN

In the supernatural scrapbook of Chester County, yet another story has taken its place among the most investigated, and publicized ghost stories in Pennsylvania.

"People were afraid of her, and the house grew to have the reputation of being haunted. But people who knew Priscilla Robinson deny these strange stories. Perhaps she was just a disappointed, cross old woman."

The words are those of Mary G. Croasdale, as published in the *Tredyffrin-Easttown History Club Quarterly* in April, 1939.

In that same publication nearly fifty years later, another writer pointed with certain pride that of six ghostly sites publicized by Pennsylvania's tourist department (including the "Ticking Tombstone," as de-

93

tailed in another chapter of this book), two–Priscilla Robinson and General Wayne (also in this book) were rooted in Tredyffrin-Easttown.

And, despite the best efforts of Mary G. Croasdale to soft-pedal the Priscilla Robinson ghost story, it has survived for well over a century.

Indeed, the story has leaped from parchment to the internet, with a few stops in books and newspaper articles along the way.

So, who was this Priscilla Robinson and why is everybody saying such terrible things about her?

According to one of the most recent and reliable sources, the Van Leer family web site, Priscilla was one of three daughters of Mary Van Leer and Moses Moore.

At the time of their marriage in 1783, the Moores resided in and operated the Blue Ball Tavern, which Mary inherited from her father, Dr. Bernardhus Van Leer.

In turn, Priscilla inherited the tavern (a.k.a. *inn*) from her parents.

Priscilla was tough. Priscilla was mean. Priscilla took no guff from no man, woman, beast or...railroad, as you will soon learn.

Said to have had a fiery temper and, uh, colorful vocabulary, Priscilla was also said to have, in her later years, a fair spread of whiskers on her chin.

Hard and hirsute, Priscilla Robinson nonetheless was more likely to answer to the unlikely nickname "Prissy."

Prissy also apparently got the last laugh on most people who may have upset her over the years. She did so simply by outliving them. She died at the age of 100 years, five months, nine days.

According to the Van Leer web site, Prissy married Edward Robinson, and then John Cahill, and then John Fisher.

Exactly what became of those men following their partings from Prissy remains vague.

"At least six skeletons have been found buried in a back room of the tavern," the author noted. "Three of them may be Prissy's three husbands–all of whom mysteriously disappeared."

The Van Leer site mentions the Tredyffrin-Easttown History Club and provides a link to the Tredyffrin Township site, where the story of Prissy Robinson-Cahill-Fisher and the Blue Ball Tavern is duly noted.

"Stories were told of lonely men who entered the tavern, never to be seen again," the township site says. It also mentions a little incident in which Prissy vented her anger with a certain railroad.

It was the line on which SEPTA trains still rumble just yards from the old Blue Ball Tavern.

The coming of the railroad cut deeply into the business of Prissy's place and other taverns along the "Main Line."

According to the township history, "Prissy fought back by greasing the rails with pig fat in an attempt to stop trains from making the incline to Paoli."

Another version of that story is that a train struck one of Prissy's pet calves, and she sought compensation for her loss. When the railroad refused to pay her, she took to the pig fat trick.

They paid.

Tough woman.

In an excellent encapsulation of ghost stories in the area, writer Bob Goshorn, in the *History Club Quarterly* of October, 1979, mentioned previous reports of the hauntings of the old tavern–then and now a private residence.

Goshorn alluded to Mary Croasdale (who had been quite active in Tredyffrin Township and Chester County political circles), and added that while she "officially" dismissed any notions of ghosts in the tavern, she admitted privately that odd things had happened to her in her nearly 58 years of residence there.

It is said she did confide that she heard dresser drawers open and close on their own in otherwise empty upstairs rooms. That phenomenon has been explained in imaginative speculation as Prissy Robinson opening and closing the drawers in search of clean clothing to replace the blood-soaked dress she wears in eternity.

It is blood-soaked, they say, because Prissy murdered husband number one, number two, number three, and perhaps several other men.

Did she really do this? Was Prissy a killer?

When renovations on the tavern were being done and the yard was reconfigured many years ago, six skeletons–some with cracked skulls and broken bones–were discovered.

Over the years, residents in the handsome old building have heard slow footsteps making their way up or down empty staircases. They have seen full apparitions in the old parlor. They have lost many a night's sleep because of the doors that bang and the drawers that slide open and shut.

One neighbor supposedly took a picture, a random picture, that, when developed, showed an old woman in a bonnet standing near the railroad tracks. It was the image of an old woman who was not present when the photograph was taken.

Word spread that it was a picture of Prissy, waiting to cuss out the engineer of the next train to rumble past.

Does Prissy Robinson haunt her old tavern? Maybe so.

Or maybe, her ghost strolls through the cemetery at Great Valley Presbyterian Church, where she rests, not necessarily in peace.

Ron and Carol Kehler took a stroll through the church graveyard in 1980, as they pondered whether to buy the old Blue Ball Tavern and make it their home.

They had seen that the property was up for sale, and although they knew about the Prissy legends and realized the place was, at that time, a classic "fixer-upper," they were somehow drawn to it.

As it turned out, Carol may have been lured by another mysterious force.

In order to get themselves into spiritual touch with the house they hoped to buy, they went in search of Prissy Robinson's grave in the sprawling Presbyterian cemetery just over the hill from the Blue Ball.

"Carol and I headed there," Ron Kehler said, "and we went up into the oldest section of the cemetery and parked."

The couple decided to split up and look for Prissy's tombstone. Less than a minute after they started their quest, they were rewarded.

"Carol was drawn right to it, maybe 35 feet away from where we were parked," Ron said. "In a strange way, she felt that Prissy had taken her by the hand and walked her there!"

The Kehlers did buy the house, moved in on a stormy Easter week in 1980, and have transformed it into a cozy family home. But, their more than two decades there have not been without incident and, perhaps, reminders that Prissy might be up to her tricks.

"Right after we moved in," Ron Kehler continued, "we weren't sure we had done the right thing. Neither one of us believed in ghosts, and we weren't sure we believed all the stories we had heard.

"Every shadow I saw, every light from the cars coming around the bend were a little eerie," the Lower Merion school district teacher added.

The Blue Ball Tavern

Anything that could be attributed to Prissy has been subtle, yet unsettling.

"Our oldest daughter was upstairs in the front room one night by herself, doing her homework. She told us the door swung open on its own. She got up, closed the door, and went back to work. Again, the door swung open. She closed it again. Then, a third time, that door swung open," he said.

A neighbor didn't make their early days there any easier when he told them about a particular, recognizable, rhythmic knock Prissy was said to have used whenever she came to call.

"Rap...rap...rap...," Ron demonstrated. "It was a series of three quick knocks, I was told."

"Well, I was out in the kitchen one time and I heard that knock–three quick raps–coming from the back room at the opposite side of the house. I went back and expected my neighbor to be standing at the door.

"I looked out and there was no one there. And, there was snow on the ground and no footprints in the snow!"

Another time, he was in the TV room in the original section of the house. There and then, he may have had his most vivid contact with Prissy, or any other spirit in the Blue Ball.

"I heard someone come down our stairs, walk across the wooden floor with hard-heeled shoes or boots on, and walk into the kitchen. It was as clear as could be," Ron said.

Houseguests and others have reported unusual experiences in the otherwise peaceful house.

"We've never seen anything," Ron confided. "In fact, the only person ever reported to have actually seen anything was one of the young girls who had lived here in the '30s or '40s who had been in the back room and turned around to see the vision of Prissy. Just that quickly, that vision disappeared."

The Kehlers had one other strange episode play out there. They had purchased an antique "Regulator" style wall clock from a dealer in Lancaster County.

It was the kind of clock that was a mainstay on the walls of railroad depots many years ago. It was in fine working order–until they mounted it on a wall in their home.

Although Ron was careful to ensure the clock was plumbed on the wall, it simply would not work. They took it back to the dealer, who hung it on a wall and watched with the Kehlers as it worked perfectly.

They took it back home, assured and sure that it would work, mounted it once again, and watched as it ticked and tocked only a few times and stopped dead.

Remember the story a few pages ago how Prissy Robinson and the railroad never quite saw eye-to-eye? Remember how she vowed then to "get even" with the railroad after they bypassed her tavern?

"Who knows," laughed Ron Kehler, "maybe through that clock–a railroad clock–old Prissy is still getting even!"

None of this has lessened the Kehlers' love for the place. They have erected a tasteful "Blue Ball Inn" sign in their front yard, and have worked very hard to maintain both the physical–and the psychical–heritage of the property.

"I think my wife and I are helping to preserve a piece of history here," Ron said with pride.

📖

THE DEVON DEMON

Somewhere in Devon, and time has dimmed the details of exactly where, a demonic spirit tormented one household after another as they attempted to stay on as renters of an old farmhouse.

Retrieved from an 1884 newspaper account and recalled by folklore collector Bob Goshorn, the story involves a "former inn" that stood "close to the Devon Inn, west of the station on the turnpike."

According to the item in the *Daily Local News*, the place was somewhat rundown and was rented by its owner to whomsoever could brave its idiosyncrasies.

It seems that a "small, dark man with a sallow face and a pack on his back" had been murdered in the old inn sometime around 1850. And, he had left is indelible mark on the old building.

For years, residents reported hearing the footsteps and at times even catching fleeting glimpses of the murdered man—backpack and all. And for years, residents left the place in short order—harrassed from the premises by the nocturnal footfalls and ghostly images.

"A number of credible witnesses," the article said, "assert that the measured tread of footsteps throughout the night is unmistakable."

In his 1979 article in *The History Club Quarterly*, Goshorn noted that the old haunted inn no longer existed.

But perhaps, the ghost still taunts the ground upon which whatever has replaced it.

📖

Philips Memorial Hall, West Chester University

UNIVERSITY GHOSTS

There is scarcely a student, faculty member, maintenance worker, administrator or alumnus of West Chester University who hasn't heard of or been touched in some way by Dr. Andrew Thomas Smith.

The first former WCU (then West Chester Normal School) to rise to the presidency of the college, Andrew Smith was president of his class when he graduated in 1893.

He became a Professor of Pedagogy until the death of school president Dr. G. M. Philips in 1927. Dr. Smith was appointed as Philips' successor.

There are many at WCU who believe that the serious, stern Dr. Smith might still be wandering the campus in spirit form.

His favorite haunt, so to speak, is the stately building that bears the name of his predecessor–Philips Hall.

"Andrew Thomas Smith is supposedly the person that haunts Philips Hall," said Gerald Schoelkopf, Rare Books Librarian and Archivist at WCU.

"He's usually sighted behind the stage," he continued.

A theater and library, Philips Hall stands out in Gothic opposition to many other buildings of more recent vintage on the college campus. It was built on the site of Dr. Philips' previous residence, "Green Gables," which was demolished to make room for the hall that would later bear his name.

If any structure at WCU *looks* haunted, it is Philips. And, by several accounts, it *is* haunted.

"You hear about incidents where lights go off for no reason," Schoelkopf noted. "It's blamed on Dr. Smith."

"Back in the late 1980s or early 1990s, one of the faculty members who deals with modern dance was having a production in Philips. She was talking to one of the students on the stage, but the student wasn't paying attention, she was distracted by something.

"The faculty member asked her who she was looking at. The student said 'the man in the audience.'

"When the teacher turned around, there was no one *in* the audience."

The auditorium was empty, except for...Dr. Smith.

Dr. Smith's spirit may have a vested interest in Philips Hall. When he died after serving only a year as president, his viewing and funeral service was conducted in the hall, which was then the college's new library.

Even the most skeptical faculty members cannot discount many of the stories that spin from the corridors and chambers of Philips Hall.

Students and professors alike say they are uncomfortable in certain areas of the auditorium. "I was once talking to a student who said that nobody wanted to ever be in the sound room by themselves," Schoelkopf said.

Seances have been held in the library section of Philips Hall. During these psychic readings, the temperature plummeted, the aroma of fresh flowers wafted through the room, and one individual reported a faint glowing figure beginning to materialize.

The most famous incident attributed to the haunting of Philips Hall involved a famous entertainer.

"The classic story," Schoelkopf said, "is that Dick Clark was speaking here, and the lights went off in the middle of his talk.

"They eventually got them back on, and everybody apologized to the crowd and to Clark.

"As Dick Clark was leaving the building, he pointed to a portrait on the wall and said 'that's who I saw!'"

As the story goes, the American Bandstand host and TV guru told some folks that when the lights went out, a man appeared as if out of nowhere. That man was the man in the portrait–Dr. Smith.

As we sat in the Special Collections Library of the college discussing the ghost stories, Gerald Schoelkopf opened a college history book to the section regarding Dr. Smith's term as college president.

Interesting among the anecdotes was one item that substantiated the man's reputation for being quite the stickler.

"Dr. Smith drew attention to the fact that some young ladies were not careful about lowering their window shades in the evening.

"He campaigned to lower the blinds, which was sadly noted by some campus and town voyeurs."

•

Keeping the shades down at Ramsey Hall isn't the problem. At the big dormitory across campus from Philips Hall, the concern is keeping their resident ghost from wreaking too much havoc.

Ramsey Hall, West Chester University

Will Michel, a marketing major and second-year resident assistant at Ramsey Hall, was quick to point out the first little anomaly there.

It's right inside the front door. It's a bronze plaque that honors the building's namesake, Dorothy Ramsey.

The "Shakespearean scholar, author, playwright, Asst. Professor of English, Professor Emeritus" was born in 1896, the plaque notes, and "DIED APRIL 31, 1974."

Unless there was, for that one year, an extra day tacked onto April, the plaque is worth noting.

"That's the first thing we all get told about," Michel, a native of Blackstalk, Ontario, said.

While incoming freshmen will invariably hear about that little chronological quirk, they are likely to also be warned about the ghost that may share their dorm with them.

Although there is no real reason to do so, the students who have passed through the dorm have come to identify any unusual occurrence as the handiwork of "Dorothy."

"We hear noises," Michel said, "especially on the sixth floor. You'll hear things up on the roof. It sounds like footsteps running, or things being dropped. The story is that she's running around up there, dropping things.

"The elevators often go up and down on their own in the middle of the night. Doors open and close on their own, things like that."

"I like to tell people that if they get along good with Dorothy, she'll get along good with them," Michel quipped.

Dr. Phillips Residence, State Normal School. West Chester, Pa.

Green Gables, which stood at the site of the present Philips Hall

CONVERSATION
WITH A SPIRITUALIST

February, 1882. Americans were still reeling from the assassination of their president when a most unusual man turned up on the streets of Reading.

So intriguing was this gentleman's visit to town, the *Reading Daily Eagle* accorded it front page news.

"The bags he had slung over his shoulders very like Santa Claus carries his precious packs," the article noted. "His cheeks were ruddy, eyes bright, step steady, form erect, and his smile was childlike and bland."

He was David Hetherley, described as "the well known medium and expounder of spiritualistic doctrines from northern Chester County.

It was a time not only of national grief, but also of national infatuation with spiritualism. David Hetherley was a chief proponent of the movement, and he was in town to relate tales from "the other side" and, of course, sell his almanacs.

"His papers," the *Eagle* continued, "contain the published communications of spirits. Some of these spirit authors are 1,500 years old and yet they treat modern subjects as if they were living present.

Were these papers bogus? Was David Hetherley selling merely snake-oil spiritualism? You couldn't have told that to the hundreds of individuals who truly believed he was in contact with spirits on both sides of that "other side."

Described as a "spiritualistic pilgrim," Hetherley won the trust of many followers in Chester County, and was making a loop into Berks County to win even more.

He offered cures, predictions, and revelations. Most of all, he offered a curious public what many truly believed was a direct pipeline to life after death and those who enjoy it, or are cursed by it.

"We all resurrect," he told a Penn Street gathering. "But, our spirits are in the spirit world just as soon as the separation from the body takes place. Spirits never find their way into graves. The earth is only polluted and poised by the dead bodies buried in it."

The newspaper writer noted that Hetherley must certainly, then, be in favor of cremation–another procedure that was gaining public scrutiny.

As his exhortations continued, the newspaper reported he "cast his eyes toward the ceiling and indulged in a weird and unintelligible stretch of flighty fancy that ear nor pen nor mind could not possibly follow."

What was most timely and tempting for the crowd and the reporter were Hetherley's thoughts–gleaned from his ethereal contacts–regarding the fate of Charles J. Guiteau.

Guiteau was in the United States Jail in Washington, D.C. awaiting his execution.

On the previous July 2, the lawyer and failed politician walked up to President James A. Garfield in the Washington railroad station and fired two shots into him. After what history has described as more than two months of medical bungling, the stricken president died.

Despite a vigorous defense that claimed it was the doctors' poor care that killed the 20th president, and not his gunshots, Guiteau was convicted. He was hanged on June 30, 1882.

But, Hetherley's visit to Reading was in February of that year, and the assassin was in jail and still the talk of the nation. And to the crowd of Readingites, he offered a shocking tale.

"Guiteau," Hetherley preached, "in his assassination of Garfield, was controlled by an evil spirit, and not by the Deity, as he claims.

"I have heard of that evil spirit. It is the spirit of one Dr. Parry who, when in the body, plotted to assassinate Queen Elizabeth, and he was executed for it."

Then, Hetherley shifted gears. "He says his name was Dr. Parry, but I think it must be Dr. Story. He was notorious for his cruelties in the reign of 'Bloody Mary.' He was hung in May, 1571, for high treason, and ever since then his spirit has been abroad inciting men to assassinate kings, czars, presidents, and people high rank."

As that theory rolled from his lips, someone asked Hetherley about Charles Guiteau's fate.

"In my view," he responded, "Spiritualists can make no greater mistake than to plead for mercy or leniency for Guiteau. If ever spirit devilry is to be defeated, it can only be by meeting the spirit enemies of justice, right, and truth. These spirit hell-hounds do not want Guiteau sent to them."

After wowing the crowd with his wild philosophies, Hetherley opened his sack and offered his almanacs–at 60 cents a pop–to anyone who cared to learn more about spiritualists and spiritualism.

It was just another day on his "spiritualistic pilgrimage."

•

Although it has absolutely nothing to do with the Brandywine Valley and is only vaguely related to the story you just read, there is an interesting sidebar story in regards to Charles J. Guiteau.

The cell in which Guiteau was incarcerated until he was executed made history of sorts in 1906.

It was in Cell No. 2 of the South Wing of the United States Jail in Washington that Harry Houdini made one of his most breathtaking escapes.

Houdini had claimed that he could break out of that cell with little or no problem. And, he upped the ante quite a bit.

A January 6, 1906 statement by J. H. Harris, warden of the jail, said it all:

This is to certify that Mr. Harry Houdini was stripped stark naked, thoroughly searched, and locked up in Cell No. 2.

Mr. Houdini, in about two minutes, managed to escape from that cell and then broke into the cell in which his clothing was locked-up. He then proceeded to release from their cells all the prisoners on the ground floor. There was positively no chance for any confederacy or collusion.

Mr. Houdini accomplished all the above-mentioned facts, in addition to putting on all his clothing, in twenty-one minutes.

The Eagle Tavern

EERINESS AT THE EAGLE

A tavern stood at what is now the busy corner of Route 100 and Conestoga Road since 1727. The present building, the Eagle Tavern, has been there since 1859.

According to the post office, the tavern is located in Uwchland, Pennsylvania. But, everybody around that intersection calls it "Eagle."

Over the years, the big inn has hosted everyone from the well-to-do to ne'er-do-wells. The notorious bandits, the Doane Brothers were known to frequent the place, as was Captain Fitz, a.k.a. "Sandy Flash," the highwayman of Chester County.

Nowadays, the Eagle is a comfortable restaurant and tavern where locals and passersby stop for nourishment and refreshment.

Although proprietor Lois Jones has never actually seen anything untoward in her tavern, and is an admitted "non believer," she will admit that whenever

111

she must ascend to the second floor, an eerie feeling seems to wrap around her.

That floor is not open to the public. It houses office and storage space.

And perhaps, it houses the Eagle's resident spirit.

Whenever an item mysteriously disappears and re-appears in the most unlikely place, the staff blames it on the ghost. Whenever something falls or moves mysteriously, they blame it on the ghost.

The staff believes it is the leftover energy from a woman who was a regular customer there until she was killed in a tragic snowmobile accident nearby.

They believe she is a protective, kind spirit–and to keep it that way, some employees have been known to whisper "good bye" to the woman's ghost as they lock up and go home for the night.

The Chadds Ford Inn

THE GHOSTLY CHILDREN OF THE CHADDS FORD INN

One could not write a book on hauntings in the "Brandywine Valley" without stepping just over the Chester County line to the Chadds Ford Inn.

From patriots to painters, natives to newcomers, the inn has been a refuge and resting place since 1736, when Francis Chadsey's son, John Chads, converted the family home into what has become the Chadds Ford Inn in the village of Chadds Ford.

Note that the very name of the family, and hence the town, evolved somehow from Chadsey to Chads (thanks to John, who dropped the "ey" for some reason), to Chadds (for what reason, nobody really knows).

Then again, the river that was forded at the Chads's or Chadds's place was once the Braindwine (after Andrew Braindwine, an early land owner) and is now the Brandywine (once more, for reasons unknown even to officials of the Chadds Ford Historical Society, which operates the John Chads House as a historical museum). But lo, there's also the tale that it was originally the Brandewijn River, after a brandy-carrying Dutch ship wrecked at its mouth in the mid- 17th century. And, what about the chap named Brantwyn, who lived along the river? Some believed the river was named after him!

Thankfully, this is not a history book. It is a ghost book. So, let us open the doors of the venerable waystation and discover its eternal occupants.

"It's always the same kinds of people they report," said floor manager Terri Wood. "It really makes you think!"

Those "same kinds of people" are the members of a trio of spirits who are said to haunt the Chadds Ford Inn.

Walking on its hardwood floors and within walls graced by the art of the likes of Howard Pyle, Peter Hurd, and the Wyeth family are ghosts–young and old ghosts, male and female ghosts. As many as a half-dozen ghosts in all.

The haunting hot buttons are all there at the inn. Faucets will turn themselves on, glasses will crash to the floor after gliding across a table or bar, lights will flicker on or off, doors will creak open or slam shut with no human aid.

At Chadds Ford, however, the incidents go much deeper into the realm of full apparitions, seen often and by many.

"We have a little boy that they say can be seen right at the top of the stairs on the second floor," Terri Wood continues.

That is Simon.

"The little boy wears bloomer pants and a ruffled shirt.

"Then," Ms. Wood continued, "there's a little girl dressed in an old-style dress and wearing a frilly hat."

That is Katie.

"We also have what people describe as a man looking like a sea captain–very rugged-looking with a beard."

That is, well, the Sea Captain.

"He's been seen upstairs," said Ms. Wood. Some patrons have reported seeing his face peering down from a second floor window in an empty room. He has also been seen gliding down a second-floor hallway.

The man who looks like an old sea captain is known only by that moniker. The children's names are purely arbitrary, given by a former employee.

She was one of many workers there who have been introduced in some way to the mostly innocent and innocuous apparitions.

One former waiter watched in awe as the little girl–Katie–appeared in the Hearth Room and was plainly seen on her tip-toes, struggling to light a candle on the mantle.

Another employee reported seeing the sea captain standing on the middle of the stairs and motioning as if he was lighting a pipe or cigar. As the stunned server watched intently for a precious few seconds, the apparition of the grizzled old man simply faded into the woodwork.

Terri Wood said the ancient inn can be a spooky place, especially when one is in it alone.

"When I first started here," she said, "I used to help the old owners on my day off, when the restaurant was closed. I would dust, clean the glass on the pictures on the wall, things like that.

"There was one time when I was here all by myself, cleaning the glass on the pictures. I did all of them in one room and went to another. When I went back into that first room, every picture was tipped, as if someone went through helter-skelter, making them all crooked.

"I knew I didn't tip them, and didn't know who did!"

Other than that, Terri has never had any personal experiences, but fully trusts her coworkers enough to believe that if they say they have experienced, sensed, or seen something awry, they indeed have.

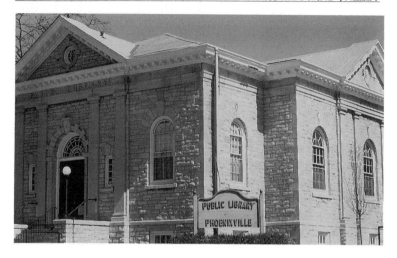

The Phoenixville Public Library

THE LADY OF THE LIBRARY

Does the gentle spirit of the first librarian in Phoenixville still wander the stacks and stairwells of the stately stone library at Second Avenue and Main Street?

Some people who toil there today believe she does.

Built with the generosity of philanthropist Andrew Carnegie in 1902, the Phoenixville Public Library remains as one of the Chester County Library System's busiest and most beautiful facilities.

And, Mary Kline, who has worked in various capacities at the library since 1995, is firmly convinced there are energies...ghosts...within the Indiana limestone walls of the building.

"I'll go into a house," Mary said of her innate ability to sense spirit activity, "and I'll know if there's ghost there. If the pressure is really nasty, I'll have to leave."

Mind you, Mary Kline is not one to dance on the edge of reality. Not at all. Mary is quite realistic about

117

her sensitivities, and despite the fact that every day she goes to work at the library she works amid the ghosts there, she has no intention of leaving.

That is simply because the energies she detects there are not in the least frightening. With the exception, perhaps, of one.

The central reading room, the Carnegie Room, remains largely unchanged from its original design. But what was a basement storage area was reconfigured in 1920 as a children's library. And that, says Mary Kline, is where she feels the strongest energies.

"When it first started," she said, "it was an older woman, maybe from around the 1890s. I believe she was between 60 and 70 years old.

"Then, a younger woman appeared. I don't know who she is, but she is much younger, maybe in her 20s."

As happens with the majority of serious paranormal experiences, Mary has never actually *seen* any floating beings, shadowy forms, or the like. She is a sensitive, and as such *feels* the spirits. It is a sensation only those who have walked in Mary's psychic shoes can fully understand.

"I just know that they're here," she added, knowing full well that some people may not really grasp what it is to sense such activity.

She added that she is not terribly shy about sharing her feelings. "Everybody here at the library knows about the ghosts and me. They either think I'm whacked, or it's OK."

One of those who believe Mary is well within the bounds of reality is John F. Kelley, the director of the Phoenixville Library. In fact, he and Mary have discussed the phenomena often, and he has proposed an identity of one of the library's spirits–and perhaps, still another.

Inside the unused former "front door" of the building is a massive plaque that honors Miss Elmira W. Pennypacker, the first director of the public library.

Could it be that her spirit still dwells there? Kelley is comfortable with that theory, as is Mary Kline. Mary has felt a presence in the Carnegie Room, and the locations of her sensations are consistent with an area where Miss Pennypacker's office would have been.

There is one more spirit in the building, much to Mary's discontent.

John Kelley believes that ghost, described by Mary as a "large, balding man," may be the residual energy of one of the members of Rev. Joseph F. Jannison's "Young Men's Literary Union," a private subscription library that was the predecessor of the public library.

But Mary shied from saying too much about, or even thinking too much about, that particular personality.

"The man," she said, obviously unnerved, "doesn't give me a comfortable feeling. I don't like the man."

Still, she goes about her duties with the knowledge that there are unseen entities in the library, perhaps keeping watch over their beloved old building and those who use it or work in it.

BOOs AT B's

As it is a barroom that's been around a while along New London Road at Landenberg, there will certainly be a good supply of "booze" at "B's Pub and Restaurant."

But, if the observations of certain patrons and workers there are to be believed, you might come across a "boo" or two at the roadhouse.

The building has served time as a hardware store, tack shop, and several incarnations as a tavern, and there's no telling the amount of human energies that may have been deposited within its walls over the years.

"I have an old picture upstairs of an old lady sitting on the front porch, and I have an odd feeling that she is one of the presences inside this building."

The words are those of Bruce Hagamon, the publican at B's. He's convinced there are certain forces at work inside his establishment.

"I know for a fact that a lot of strange things happen here," he continued. One incident, as innocent as it may seem, involved a spatula.

It is a large, commercial food service spatula that, as Bruce was entered the kitchen, started to sway back and forth at an alarming pace.

"Absolutely nothing else in this kitchen was moving except that one spatula," he assured. "It was weird."

Bruce believes the energies are centered in the kitchen and bar areas, and he is not alone in those beliefs.

"I've had people tell me they've seen things in the corner of their eye, as if someone was following them into or out of the kitchen," he added.

At least one worker there has reported seeing what she could best describe as a "gauzy looking" woman in a blue or green dress brush past her.

A bartender who preferred to remain anonymous also detected something in the basement of B's.

"For some reason, in one section down there, as soon as I turn around to leave, I feel as if I see something, as if it's following me. When I turn around, it's not there. It's a presence, or a shape of something there. It's happened to me four or five times. It's kind of an eerie feeling. I'm not scared, but there's definitely something there."

Bruce Hagamon is also unfettered by the possibility that his pub is haunted.

"I truly do believe there is something here," he said. "A lot of people talk about the ghost, or ghosts. But, when it comes right down to it, I have no problem with it."

Live and let live, so to speak.

THE HEIRESS AND THE STABLE BOY

The chapter title is not ours. We borrow it from a segment in a fine video documentary entitled "College Hauntings," which portrays ghost stories at three colleges in the Delaware Valley.

In it, producer Gary White reenacted the oft-told tale of what he described as "innocence, love, betrayal, suicide, and miscarriage" at an exclusive Main Line estate that has become a fine liberal arts college.

It is Cabrini College, to be precise.

By its own definition, Cabrini College is part of the international educational ministry of the Missionary of the Sacred Heart of Jesus.

Its name comes from Maria Francesca Cabrini (1850-1917), a frail Italian woman who emigrated to New York City and established a convent, and then an orphanage, and then a hospital. Her influence spawned many more health care and humanitarian institutions, and in 1946 she was canonized by Pope Pius XII. She was America's first saint.

The Cabrini campus is exquisite, having been the estate of Campbell Soup founder John T. Dorrance.

"Woodcrest," as the Dorrance family called it, is dominated by a 51-room Tudor mansion now called Cabrini Mansion.

Under its ornate ceiling, within its elegant chambers, and around its hidden passageways and mysterious chambers, the mansion holds many secrets.

Much of what was the essence of family life at Woodcrest was removed when the estate became a college in 1957. The Dorrance family quarters are now administrative offices. The beautifully landscaped "yard" is now a college campus.

But, some believe there are other "essences" of family life at Woodcrest that remain very much in the present at Cabrini College.

Students, faculty, and administrators there have repeated the ghost stories of Cabrini College for many years. They have made their way onto the pages of many books and articles, and every story follows the same basic scenario—a scenario presented centuries ago by a writer named Shakespeare in a story called "Romeo and Juliet."

The ghostly lineup at Cabrini includes a young girl, a young boy, and an old man. Their identities remain a mystery, but it is generally accepted that they are spirits from the Woodcrest days.

Exactly whose ghosts are there is also a stew of speculation. Some believe the young girl's ghost is that of the mansion owner's daughter. The young boy's spirit is that of a stable boy, or the carriage master's son. The older man is the master of the estate himself.

Open even wider for arbitration is just how those energies were imprinted there.

A campus folklorist told the story of how the master of the estate discovered that his daughter was getting a bit too friendly with the stable boy and cut off their budding romance.

The boy went into what is now Grace Hall and hanged himself.

The girl leaped from the balcony in the mansion in her suicide plunge.

Another version, also espoused by the folklore of the college, has it that the young woman (the heiress) was made pregnant by the young man (the stable boy). Fully aware that the child would never be accepted into the family, she killed it and buried it somewhere on the property.

As for the older man? He is supposedly none other than the girl's father.

A 2000 graduate of Cabrini, who asked that we not use her name, learned all the stories (as most incoming freshmen do) when she started at Cabrini, but swears that none of them influenced her later into her college days there when she actually encountered two of the three school ghosts.

"She was wearing a light blue, illuminated kind of dress," the woman said of the little girl. Even more bizarre was another observation made. "She didn't have any feet!"

"Yeah, I thought that was strange," she admitted.

"I was taking a walk late at night to clear my head. It was one of the ways I relieve stress and tension. I was walking past Woodcrest, near where the baby is said to be buried.

"It seemed as if she was communicating to me, asking me where her baby was. I just kind of blew it off, like, this can't be happening!"

She told only one other person of the incredible event, fearing ridicule by anyone who may not understand. "They'd think I was bizarre," she said.

The Cabrini grad looks back on her years there as pleasant. The campus, the curriculum, the people–all are top-notch, she said.

Having said that, however, she went on to describe her second meeting with one of the ghosts there.

"I believe I met the little girl's father," she said. "He was wearing a top hat and a black overcoat, typical of a man in the early part of the last century.

"He just turned around, looked at me, and I asked if I could help him.

"I could see right through him. I knew it wasn't an actual person.

"Then, he just turned around again and faded away as he walked from me."

The Cabrini alumna insisted that what she said she saw, she saw.

"But I don't discuss it much at all," she concluded. "Let's face it, a lot of people will think of me as being very strange. I didn't purposely go out and try to contact these spirits, they just came to me."

BEANIE

The building along the west branch of the Brandy-wine at Mortonville has been a general store, a barber shop, and, if tantalizing tales are to be believed, a brothel.

These days, it's Dugal's Inn, a comfortable restaurant with charming country décor.

And...Beanie.

Beanie once owned the 100-plus year old building and, its present owners said, was quite a character. He was perhaps best known as a stickler about loudness and rowdiness. It was not unusual for him to ask folks to leave if they got too noisy.

That could very well be why everybody at Dugal's now attributes certain occurrences to Beanie's spirit.

"My sister and I were sitting here at the bar," said bartender Rainy Carlin, "and she had pulled the plug on the juke box. All of a sudden, the jukebox turned itself on and played the Irish song 'Wild Colonial Boy.'

"Now, when the jukebox is plugged in, it can sometimes start up on its own. But I went over to check. That plug was pulled!"

Almost everything blamed on Beanie involves noise.

"Another night," Carlin added, "there was blue-grass music playing when somebody shouted out 'Shut up! Be quiet!'"

Carlin noted, however, that the place was empty at the time. "It came out of nowhere," he said.

Cynthia Sanderson is the bar manager and sister of the owner. "There was one evening I was bartending and the band was setting up its equipment. The TV

126

was off, but plugged in. The band's amps were not yet plugged in.

"All of a sudden, out of nowhere, we heard a very gruff 'Turn down!'

"Everybody at the bar heard it, and they tried to rationalize it. But, we could do nothing but blame it on Beanie."

Various other electrical-based anomalies are fairly regular happenings at Dugal's. But what happened to hostess Hillary Shaver one time may indicate that Beanie may have a ghostly accomplice.

"I was in the dining room with the other waitresses. We were setting tables. There was one couple in there and the lady looked at us and asked us about the history of the restaurant.

"She asked us if there were any ghosts here. She had a very solemn look on her face. Then, she wanted us to tell her about the 'lady's ghost.'

"Well, we said we didn't actually have a *lady* ghost. As a matter of fact, the ghost was a man we called 'Beanie.'

"She said there was a ghost in the ladies room. She said she had gone into the ladies room and when she opened the back stall she saw the silhouette of someone in the stall, but when she looked more closely, there was no one there.

"Her boyfriend had walked her to the bathroom because she didn't know where it was, and he told her that when he took her there, he felt a sharp chill go through his body."

Cynthia Sanderson, who once lived on the third floor of the building, said she often had feelings that she was not alone up there.

Servers have reported doors opening and closing on the second floor, and some employees won't go up there alone. "It weirds me out," exclaimed one employee.

THE CASE OF THE DISAPPEARING B&B GUEST

It was midday when I walked up the driveway to the side entrance of the lovely Tudor home in Phoenixville.

Chaim Chachkes was tending to his host chores by welcoming a guest who had pulled in the driveway just minutes earlier. In the shadows of the sycamores along Virginia Avenue in Phoenixville, the young lady unloaded her bags from her car as I unloaded what turned out to be a very *loaded* question.

The affable Mr. Chachkes smiled when I introduced myself and asked about the ghost I had learned inhabited their ca. 1927 charmer.

Before he could go into detail in regards to my quest, he helped the young woman with her luggage and led her to her room.

When the house is not just the Chachkes' home, it becomes The Manor House bed and breakfast.

The incoming guest seemed startled when she heard my question. "Ghosts? Here?," she asked, a look of genuine concern on her face. "And I'm staying here for three nights? With ghosts?"

I assured her that she had nothing to worry about. The reported spirits of the Manor House were *good* ghosts. I appealed to her basic senses.

Or, so I had hoped.

I reckoned she was feigning fear. She would settle in, realize what a wonderful place it is, and maybe even revel in the reality that gentle spirits may watch over her as she spent those three quiet nights there.

We parted company. She, along with Chaim up the red oak staircase to the third floor–the former maids' quarters–where her room was situated. I, past the Chickering parlor grand piano, between extraordinary pieces of art and antiques and into a comfortable couch in the sitting room.

Chaim came downstairs after showing the woman her accommodations. He told me she seemed sincerely spooked by the notion of ghosts. He shrugged it off.

As the guest went about her business upstairs, Chaim related some of the tales that have been told about the place. But, it was his wife, Harriet, who could better tell them. She was at her part-time job at the Phoenixville Public Library, but I could contact her later in the day.

As it turned out, I "met" Harriet first via email, and it was from the subject line of her correspondence that I derived the title of this chapter.

"You may be amused (we were) that our three-day B&B guest who overheard the tale (1) moved downstairs to be closer to us, and (2) shortened her stay by two days, and (3) checked out sometime between midnight and five the next morning!" Harriet wrote.

The skittish guest should not have been concerned. The spirits of Chaim and Harriet's house are gentle, and only occasionally make themselves evident.

They are the rare but real types of spirits that may have been imprinted in the house without the act of a death.

A preponderance of evidence suggests that certain "ghosts," or, more properly, *energies*, may be "deposited" by intense emotional or physical release, not exclusively limited to the passing of a life.

In fact, the human energies and emotions expended in the joyous celebration of life can find their way onto certain repositories and emerge in the psychic mind as passive or residual entities. They are, of course, not "ghosts," in the classic interpretation, but do provide the aberrations attributed to "hauntings."

Also, it is believed by some researchers and investigators that this energy discharged from living beings can even be "recorded" and then transported from one place to another on furniture or building materials.

Neither Chaim nor Harriet can accurately trace the source of the activities in their Manor House.

The faint sound of laughing children has been heard by several guests. The laughter is detected mostly at the foot of the attic stairs.

The other presence in the Chachkes' home is best described as "The Red-Headed Woman."

Not long ago, a guest came down for breakfast and seemed a bit confused. Harriet asked her what was wrong.

The guest told her that she was a bit put off when, she believed, someone came into her room, stood at the foot of the bed, and shook her legs until she awakened.

The woman thought it was Harriet. It was not. In fact, as she looked more closely at Harriet and recalled her odd experience, she realized it *couldn't* have been Harriet. Harriet would never do such a thing.

The woman, who insisted that she was fully awake and aware at the time, said she looked up to gaze upon her intruder and noticed nothing other than her brilliant red hair.

Harriet does not have red hair.

But, a previous mistress of the mansion did.

She also had eight children.

•

Chaim and Harriet Chachkes have opened their Virginia Avenue Tudor several times for tours of the most beautiful homes in Phoenixville.

Among others homes on those tours was a home with the dubious distinction of being known locally as "The Blob House."

While that may sound a bit disconcerting, those out of the Phoenixville loop should know that it earned that moniker when the foyer of the 3rd and Main Sts. building was used in the 1958 science fiction movie, "The Blob."

Which in a curious way brings us to our next story.

The Inn at Historic Yellow Springs

CHILLS AT CHESTER SPRINGS

Irwin ("Shorty") Yeaworth held a capacity crowd captive at a Phoenixville Historical Society program.

His topic for this august grouping of historians and cultural icons of the community?

A blob.

"*The* Blob," to be precise–the 1958 drive-in classic movie that sent places like Pottstown, Downingtown,

132

and Phoenixville (where scenes were shot) into a film frenzy.

It also launched the career of a young actor named Steve McQueen.

Some attendees at the meeting were there to talk film.

Q: What was it like to work with Steve McQueen?

Yeaworth: He wasn't Steve McQueen yet, if you know what I mean. Ha!, he was probably asked what it was like to work with Shorty Yeaworth!

Some were there to rehash old times.

Q: Do you remember your time in Phoenixville?

Yeaworth: "Sure. It's an unusual community, a true 'town.' The fact that it's off the beaten track is one reason it's retained its small-town character.

I was there to talk ghosts. Specifically, the ghosts of Chester Springs.

Known alternately as Yellow Springs, the village was Shorty Yeaworth's "Hollywood on the Pickering" as he and a dedicated community of artisans eked out a living and created several true cinematic gems.

Yeaworth, who directed "The Blob" and two other films of the genre, "4-D Man" and "Dinosaurus," said

133

he and about 50 others lived in communal style in the 18 buildings of Chester Springs. They worked under the name of "Good News Productions." When they weren't producing horror movies, they were producing religious films.

Times were tough, but interesting. They were not above taking handouts from Philadelphia-area Rescue Missions, and as the seeds of their creativity blossomed, they worked hard to harvest the fruit.

They were a resourceful lot. In the filming of "The Blob," for example, Shorty rented a 35-millimeter camera for three weeks. To maximize its use, filming generally went on 24 hours a day, seven days a week

Later to become involved in commercial and industrial productions, Yeaworth enthusiastically recalled those days in Chester Springs, and was proud to note that he helped to put Chester County on the horror movie map.

Reasoning that a man who dared to step out of the Hollywood box to produce "monster movies" must have an appreciation for the paranormal, I posed my question:

Q: Were there any ghost stories to come out of your days at Chester Springs?

Yeaworth: Oh, yes. There were many tales about the old "Washington Building." I remember several people talking about rattling, clattering sounds up on the third and fourth floors.

The Washington Building is now an elegant restaurant, and the cluster of buildings from whence "The Blob" blubbered is now Historic Yellow Springs. It is one of Chester County's historical treasures.

Well before the rumbles of revolution began to rattle in southeastern Pennsylvania, many folks were finding their way into the cozy glen not far from the Pickering Creek.

By 1750, the attractions of the mineral springs there and the supposed "cures" they offered became so strong that an enterprising hotelier named Robert Pritchard secured a license and opened the first tavern near the springs.

The natives of that glen had already established those bubbling waters as mystical and curative, but the incursion of the settlers transformed the site into one of America's first health spas.

As the revolutionary rumbles swelled into war, the tranquility of the resort was disturbed at the order of none other than George Washington.

In 1777, Washington commissioned construction of a substantial building that would be the only hospital to specifically serve the encampment at Valley Forge.

After that noble service, Yellow Springs returned as a spa resort, rivaling those at Saratoga Springs, N.Y., and Newport, R.I.

And then, another war broke out in 1860 and the old hospital was recomissioned until those hostilities between the states ended.

Following the Civil War, an orphanage for soldiers' children was opened there. A few decades later, the site was "discovered" by the arts and crafts crowd.

Art schools and galleries were established, the Pennsylvania Academy of the Arts opened a summer camp there, and The Blob was born there.

Remnants of almost every transition made in this bucolic crease of land can be seen in the 145-acre property administered by Historic Yellow Springs, Inc., a non-profit organization formed in 1974.

The most striking historical remnant is the ruin of the old Continental Army Hospital. Once taller than three stories, the hospital's foundations and low stone walls are all that remain.

Buildings on the grounds house art galleries, art schools, and residences. And, in a meadow that ex-

135

tends from the village to the creek are the locations of the iron, sulfur, and magnesium springs that brought early visitors (said to have included Jenny Lind, Daniel Webster, Henry Clay and three presidents) to the remote valley.

It is in the Yellow Springs Inn, the charming descendant of Pritchard's 1750 hotel, where a spiral of ghostly energy swirls.

Jeff Merkel, one of the managers of the inn, has found himself in the vortex of that spiral, and came away with a sighting of one of the spirits of the elegant restaurant.

Jeff's up-close-and-personal meeting with the ghost took place in the second-floor Victorian Room, one of many romantic dining rooms of the inn.

He came through the door into the room when he saw, in front of the fireplace, what he initially believed to have been a dog.

That, of course, would have been a bit out of the ordinary. But, Jeff could not have imagined just how extraordinary it would all become.

As he focused on the object, he saw that it was not a dog at all.

It was a little boy.

Astonished and confused as to who the boy was and why he was there, Jeff had little time to reason. It seemed that when the boy, dressed in what Jeff remembers as a black coat, noticed Jeff, he panicked.

Jeff swore that the boy straightened up from his hunched position by the fireplace and darted toward a wall.

Along the way, the little boy vanished. Poof! Disappeared.

Jeff was stunned. He could not then, and cannot now believe that what he saw was real. Yet, he knows it was. It was a little boy...who disappeared in a flash.

136

As he tried to come up with some sort of explanation, he could only figure that the little boy's presence there may have had something to do with the era when a part of the village was the Soldiers' Orphans School.

Maybe, just maybe, the little boy in the Victorian Room was an orphan who either decided to or was somehow destined to remain as an eternal resident of the building.

There have been many other unexplainable or odd incidents in other rooms of the inn. Jeff recalled a time when a serving tray he had just set up lifted, as if by unseen precision, and flipped as both he and his customers watched. It wasn't gravity, it wasn't a bump—one end of the tray simply lifted up, and the other end went tumbling.

The inn is the site of several Elderhostel programs throughout the year, and at one of them, the program organizer approached Jeff.

She told him that one of the women in the group had told her that she had been pestered by the presence of two children who approached her during the program.

The program chairwoman thought the woman had either imagined or manufactured the story. She chuckled about it, and dismissed it as the ramblings of a little old lady.

Jeff Merkel did not.

THE SINGING SPIRIT
OF HURRICANE HILL

Should you be enjoying a fine *Filet au Poivre, Trout en Parch*, or *Lobster Fra Diavola* at the Crier in the Country restaurant and hear the faint echo of someone softly singing, do not be alarmed.

It's probably Lydia.

Perhaps it is *Veal Alphonse* you are having when you see a chandelier begin to sway back and forth.

It's probably Lydia.

Alternatively, maybe, you're enjoying a rack of lamb when a grayish blur passes silently in front of you.

Lydia.

Much human drama has played out within the walls of the disarmingly charming restaurant along Route 1 in Glen Mills, Delaware County. Many people have lived there over more than two and a half centuries, and perhaps one or two of them have never left.

One of them is Lydia.

The first home on the second-highest point in Delaware County, known locally as "Hurricane Hill," was built in 1740 by Thomas Pennell. The oldest portion of the Crier in the Country, the rear bar and kitchen, were part of that home.

It was in 1861 when Thomas P. Powel built the core of the present Victorian structure. There, he and his wife, Lydia Powel, resided in their opulent country mansion along the busy Baltimore Pike.

138

Henry E. Saulnier purchased the property from Lydia Powel following her husband's death, and it was Saulnier who expanded and improved the mansion during his family's tenure there from 1873 to 1916.

After several turnovers in ownership, the Powel Mansion was bought by the Iannucci family and converted into an elegant restaurant, the Crier in the Country. The name came was inspired by owner Jerry Iannucci's longtime Upper Darby restaurant, the Town Crier.

In late 1995, brothers Joseph and Robert Jackson took ownership, and have maintained the high level of quality of both cuisine and atmosphere.

And with that atmosphere came a ghost or two.

On their menu, the Jacksons say: "If you close your eyes you can almost hear the clopping of horse-drawn carriages passing, the clinking of glasses, and the laughter of those who have enjoyed the grandeur of this home before us."

All very well—but if you close your eyes, you just might miss catching a fleeting glimpse of Lydia, or any of the other spirits that swirl around inside the Crier.

Tales of hauntings up on Hurricane Hill go back at least to the 1960s when odd things started happening and odd sights started showing up during the building's existence as the Fox Crest Inn. Stories of its haunting spread throughout the area.

But, the happenings and sights intensified when Jerry Iannucci purchased the place.

In fact, it was in the very first week of his opening of the Crier in December, 1983 when Incident One of a long list of incidents unfolded.

It took place, as it turned out, in an upstairs room they have named in honor of Lydia Powel. It is the most, but not only, haunted room in the restaurant.

A waitress was passing through the Lydia Room when she was stopped in her tracks by an icy chill. In the otherwise comfortable room, a stiff blast of cold air seemed to wrap around her. It was so cold, she said, that she could see her breath.

As she stood agape, the blast of wind–which by her reckoning could not have come from any logical source–seemed to blow its way through the door, down the hall and to a back door. It was so powerful, the waitress recalled, that it nearly pushed the door off its hinges.

Another employee, a janitor, has reported the sound of singing coming from the Lydia Room. Not once, but several times, he was distracted by the melodies, walked toward the Lydia Room to check on who might be inside, and was accosted by what he could describe only as a "gray flash" that drifted swiftly in front of him.

There is a consensus at the Crier that Lydia Powel's spirit remains there. "And if we did something that didn't please her, she'd let us know."

Jerry Iannucci himself has had some experiences that have put him on guard.

The most incredible was when he came into the Powel Room, a main dining room, only to see a massive chandelier on the ceiling swaying rhythmically. The longer he watched, the more violent the swaying. It got to the point that he had to step in and stop the movement. It took all he had to bring the swinging chandelier to a halt.

A waitress told Jerry that she noticed the chandelier start to sway just after a patron had asked her if there were any ghosts in the restaurant.

The staff and several customers have reported numerous incidents. Jerry's own son and daughter-in-law, who once resided in the mansion for a short time, would hear the sound of laughter, clinking glasses, and general gaiety in the main part of the restaurant as they sat in their third-floor loft residence.

As the Iannuccis' introduction to the energies at the old mansion came shortly after their occupation of it, so did the Jacksons'.

The Iannuccis were retiring, and Robert and Joseph Jackson were about to take possession of the restaurant in November, 1995.

Two days before the day of the settlement, a storm propelled by winds of up to 75 miles per hour swept across Hurricane Hill and felled two ancient trees that stood in front of the mansion.

They were "sentinel trees," planted by the Powels in a neat ring around their house.

They had grown to become tall and strong. But, they were no matches for the howling gales of November, 1995. Two of the tallest fell like dominoes.

Was it a gust...or a ghost?

Of course, Lydia Powel could not control the weather. She could not have ordered up the maelstrom that mangled the sentinel trees.

But, both the buyers and sellers of the property that day marveled at the coincidence.

Jerry Iannucci noted that Lydia was forced to sell her beloved estate at auction. It was a painful, gut-wrenching decision for her. "We don't think she wanted to leave," he said.

At the time of the tree-toppling, Cissie Iannucci, Jerry's wife and partner, lamented that maybe Lydia didn't want *them* to leave.

The Jackson brothers and their staff have had their own dealings with Lydia. Robert told of servers who late at night set up tables for banquets the next day, left the place, and returned the next morning to find every place setting very much out of place. The silverware was neatly stacked in the middle of the table. The napkins were unfolded and piled high. Every ta-

141

ble they set was un-set by, they truly believed, Lydia Powel's mischievous ghost.

Of the several stories reported by patrons who knew nothing of Lydia's alleged spirit there, one stands out as particularly interesting.

A gentleman had been using the upstairs men's room and as he prepared to return to his table, he had a most unnerving experience.

As he stood at the sink washing his hands, he happened to look into the mirror. He was riveted in place as to his shock he saw, quite clearly in the reflection, a woman in Victorian dress standing just over his shoulders.

It shook him. But, in a second or so he realized it had to have been a painting or, by some weird chance, a costumed woman who accidentally wandered into the men's room.

In an instant, he turned and looked over his shoulder. The room was empty. There was no painting on the wall, and no costumed woman.

He returned to his table to tell his companions and his waiter of his strange, frightening encounter in the men's room. He dismissed it all as the workings of his imagination.

He was forced to rethink that and reassess the entire matter after he learned for the first time about the restless ghost of Lydia Powel, who may have come to call on that man in that room on that night on Hurricane Hill.

📖

THE "BLACK ARTS" AND "IMAGINARY CRIMES"

There has been an uneasy coexistence of fact and fancy regarding the supernatural in Chester County and the areas on its fringes.

As referenced elsewhere in this volume, folklorist J. Alden Mason once urged "The collection and study of local folklore is a field that by no means should be neglected by historical organizations."

About 50 years after Mason's declaration, Wesley L. Sollenberger and Rosemary Philips, in their 1988 "One Hundred and One Answers to One Thousand and One Questions," published by the Chester County Historical Society, noted: "There is little information on witchcraft/haunted houses/inns, etc. The Quakers were for the most part very practical and few Quakers believed in witchcraft or haunted houses."

Quite true, perhaps. But, those early Quaker settlers were not without their superstitions and were not immune to the folk beliefs of those around them.

It was in Chester and Delaware counties that the earliest reports of the "black arts" came to the attention of the people, the courts, and the church leaders of a very young colony of Pennsylvania.

A full 18 years before the more famous Salem, Massachusetts, witchcraft hysteria, a Delaware County woman was brought before William Penn himself and charged with what author George Smith, M.D., called "the imaginary crime of witchcraft."

Dr. Smith made reference to the trial of "the Witch of Ridley Creek," Margaret Mattson.

143

In her humble homestead along the stream, Margaret allegedly bewitched cows and engaged in certain practices that seemed to violate the 1603 English law that defined witchcraft and made the practice of same punishable by death.

During her trial in 1684, it is said that Penn asked the Swedish woman, point-blank, if she was a witch–if she had ever ridden across the sky on a broomstick. Through an interpreter, Mattson supposedly answered "yes" and "yes" to the queries.

For whatever reason, the proprietor of the colony declared the woman "not guilty" and allowed her to return to her home.

Eleven years after the Mattson trial, another incident titillated folks in the Brandywine Valley.

It was announced at the October, 1765 meeting of the Concord Monthly Meeting of Friends that several of their number, members of the John Roman family, were suspected of practicing "astroligy (sic) and other sciences, as Geomancy and Cliorvmancy (sic) Necromancy, etc."

Allegations and denials followed as a committee of Friends' investigators probed the Romans' case. It was further discovered that John, Philip, and Robert Roman had used divining rods and had engaged in "Rabdomancy."

The matter eventually landed in the hands of a "Grand Inquest by the King's Authority" in Chester County. That Grand Jury sided with the Friends and fined Robert Roman five pounds. He was also ordered to "never practice the Arts, but behave himself well for the future." Upon paying the fine and agreeing to the terms, Roman was allowed to return home.

In these earliest years of the Pennsylvania Colony, stories of these heinous crimes peppered the pages of gazettes and court proceedings. Although the Margaret Mattson affair has been called "Pennsylvania's only witchcraft trial," there is ample evidence to suggest it was not.

There is no doubt that the Quakers had little tolerance for practitioners of the "black arts." A decision rendered by the Goshen Monthly Meeting in March, 1750, also proved that they disdained any acts of their own number who attempted to exact their own punishment on suspicious neighbors.

In that meeting, member Robert Jones was disowned by the congregation. He was accused and censured for harassing a woman "believed to be a witch," "driving her from her home," and "otherwise abusing her."

On the subject of collection of folklore in Chester County, one individual comes to the fore. Dr. Daniel G. Brinton, (1837-1899) former president of the American Folklore Society, published an impressive array of folk beliefs and stories in the society's journal in 1892.

The Thornbury native offered thoughts and theories on death and spirit energies. He suggested that at the time of death, the departure of the spirit might be accompanied by a buzzing sound or some sort of physical manifestation.

He touched on how energy imprints could be made and, thus, how a place could be "haunted." He even recalled certain areas from his Chester County childhood where ghosts were said to roam.

In Delaware County, an early reference volume and repository for ghostly goodies is Henry Graham Ashmead's 1884 *History of Delaware County, Pennsylvania.*

Accessible at libraries, or in its entirety on the internet, Ashmead's effort provides 19th century tidbits that serve as tantalizing morsels for 21st century hunters of hauntings.

He wrote about the area of the "White Horse level, on the Queen's Highway, through Ridley," where might be seen "the ghost of Luke Nethermarke, who, about the middle of the last century, in galloping his horse at night amid the storm and the darkness as he hastened homeward, rode into a tree which had been blown down by the gale and was killed."

He mentioned a "phantom sentinel" from the Revolutionary War era who still strolls the streets of Chester...a specter named Moggey, who could be spotted at Knowlton, rising from her grave...the ghost of a peddler murdered at Munday's Run...the "slain woman who made the archway of the old granary at Chester a spot to be avoided after dusk"...and an evil spirit–a "caco-demon"–who dwelled in the cellar of the old school house at Welsh and Fifth Streets.

"Narration of the terrible and supernatural," Ashmead called it.

Old traditions, superstitions, and stories die hard. While researching this book, a writer self-described only as "An ancient Chester County teacher" thought we might like to know that a horseshoe tacked to his front door in 1910 is still there, still a magnet for good luck.

The writer added, "As children, we were taught the following song,"

I found a horseshoe, I found a horseshoe!
I picked it up and nailed it on the door.
It was rusted and full of nails,
But it brought good luck to me, evermore!

📖

A FIRE HOUSE EXORCISM

This is a story about a place that is not haunted, an exorcism that was more symbolic than psychic and "spirit" rather than spirits.

I believe it warrants inclusion in this volume for two reasons.

First, the news account from the Associated Press has been in my files since November, 1989. The actual story, ripped from the wire service when I was in the news department of a Reading radio station has yellowed and frayed over the years, but I promised myself then that if I ever did a book on ghosts in Chester County, I would track the story down.

Secondly, it is a bit of light relief amid the dark stories of this book as well as a testimony to the respect and sensitivity one segment of our society feels for those who have come before them.

Legends and ghost stories at fire stations are common. Are there ghosts in the house of the First West Chester Fire Company in East Bradford Township? More than likely, yes.

And if there are, that's just fine with the volunteers there.

The news item of November 9, 1989, sets the stage:

"When the First West Chester Fire Company moved into its new headquarters, it didn't leave anything in the old building, not even the ghosts of former firefighters.

"'The old building is over 100 years old and the deceased members are supposedly still living there,' said Fred Criscuolo, the assistant fire chief.

"In order to 'move' the ghosts, firefighters wore tags with the names of deceased company members during relocation ceremonies."

It should be obvious why that item stirred my curiosity.

Fred Criscuolo went on to serve as the company's chief for three years, and still volunteers at the station, even in "semi-retirement."

His passions for not only the First West Chester, but for the traditions of fire fighting are obvious.

Tradition is something the members of First West Chester know very well. It was founded in 1799 and is the oldest of the West Chester Fire Department's three companies.

The building the company vacated in 1989 was in the heart of the county seat, across from the courthouse.

"The fire company was there for so many years," Fred noted, "that the older members thought the spirits of the fire company were still there. So, we actually moved them to our new fire station."

They did so in a most demonstrative fashion–one that made nationwide news.

"We had a bunch of fire fighters get together and we sort of chased them out and into a fire truck and drove them to the new firehouse," Fred remembered.

"It was very noisy. We had a smoke machine we use for training, and we filled the firehouse full of smoke. We had firefighters go in and rattle pots and pans and make some noise."

Some members were dressed in vintage firefighting clothing, some of that garb dating back as far as 150 years.

It was all representative of not necessarily the spirits–as in ghostly spirits–of the deceased brethren, but of the spirit they left behind.

148

"I truly believe that spirit of those men was there," the former chief said. He further believes that there are certain things that happen at the "new" fire station that seem to happen because of that spirit.

Tasks are completed as if guided by an invisible helping hand or two. "It's hard to put into words," Fred continued. "Things just get done that shouldn't have gotten done, if you know what I mean.

"We still have members who are 80 years old who come up once a month and sit around. To me, there's a reason for that; there's some attraction there. And, I've been doing it for 27 years and I still go up there like a new kid. I have to believe that there is a reason for it. It's not a 'haunting' thing, you know, but it was always a great place to hang around, and maybe the spirits of some of the old guys are still hanging around."

The historical motto of the First West Chester Fire Company is "Faithful and Fearless." That saying may also apply to both the past and present members of the proud unit.

Did the 1989 stunt release the spirits of all past members from their old digs? Did any ghosts of firefighters past miss the truck?

Ask a Moose!

It's easy to spot the old fire station on Church Street, across from the courthouse in West Chester. Because it is on the historic register, its façade could not be changed.

Today, it is a Moose lodge hall. Do any phantoms from the ranks of the "Faithful and Fearless" still hang out there?

Ask a Moose!

SPIRITS OF THE HORSESHOE

Buzzards Rock...Goat Hill...An ancient Indian village...bootleggers and moonshiners...ruins of an old church...murder...*ghosts*...

These are images that swirl within the sprawling bounds of a collection of scout camps divided by the geographic anomaly known as "The Horseshoe."

It is the horseshoe (actually a double, even triple horseshoe) of the Octoraro River in extreme southwestern Chester County.

Actually, the scout camps along the looping banks spread into five townships, three counties, and two states.

Wilmer W. MacElree, a former Chester County District Attorney and Judge, wrote in his 1934 Around the Boundaries of Chester County:

"Below Wood's Bridge the Octoraro meanders around the southwestern corner of West Nottingham Township and flows into Maryland; then loath to leave the state that gave it birth it turns northward once again and lingers long enough to murmur its farewell and having done so hastens on its quest for the Susquehanna."

So finicky is the stream that there is one section of the scout reservation that was named "No County Bottom." When the Octoraro changed course several years ago, it also affected the boundaries of properties, counties, and even states. For some time, nobody was sure exactly what county or state a small portion of the land between the loops was situated in!

It is a fascinating piece of Chester County (and Lancaster and Cecil counties), Pa. (and Md.), and a

150

treasured and storied land where thousands of young people in the Scouting movement have had many adventures.

Some of those adventures involved ghosts.

There are several legends that raise the flames of campfires in the Horseshoe.

In the camp's historical documents, much tribute is paid to the natives who occupied the region long before the Scouts opened their camp there on July 19, 1928.

According to Rev. Edward B. "Casey" Jones and Louis Lester, early camp leaders and historians, those natives were the Octoraros; a subtribe of Lenni-Lenapes whose settlement there included a village called Shawana.

Much of the history of Camp Horseshoe is speculative, but the legends live on.

Lester: *The site of old Shawana Town cannot be far away. With such a stimulant to fancy it would not surprise me if a youthful scout of imaginative vision were to see in the dusk of evening some flitting wraiths of Shawnee warriors among the rocks and the trees of this long, wild, wooded ravine.*

Jones: *The spirit of the Horse's Hoof is today the Spirit of the Horseshoe...and often on a summer evening he returns to this sacred spot, where we stand, and gives his blessing to all who hear him...in the voice of the birds, of the rain, and in the gentle nestle of the trees; the Spirit of the Horseshoe is ever about us.*

These wonderful images aside, there is cause to believe that ghosts of more recent and real vintage may glide within the great horseshoe bend of the Octoraro.

For 29 years, Ernie Heegard was the director of Camp Horseshoe. The former Willistown Township resident spoke to us from his current home in Cape May, N.J. He was well acquainted with the legends of

151

the camp, and even more familiar with the recurring ghost story of one of the camp's landmark buildings.

"Our first camp ranger was C.C. Coley," Heegard said. "He was brought in from Alberta, Canada, to clear the area behind the Conowingo Dam before they flooded the area."

According to camp history, Coley lived in what has become known as the "White House."

"The story goes that there were two brothers who owned the house before he took over," according to Heegard. "Those two brothers had gotten into a real knock-down, drag-out feud.

"One of them left the house, but one night he came back, accosted the other, and one of them was killed."

In an historical narrative, former Chief Scout Executive Louis Lester corroborated Ernie Heegard's recollections, with slight revisions.

Lester said the "White House" was occupied by three bachelor brothers named Taylor. He wrote, "One of them disappeared many years ago in a very mysterious fashion. It was common gossip in the neighborhood that he was killed by the other two men and buried back of the pump."

And, Lester noted that the victim might still be hanging around the Horseshoe.

"His ghost is supposed to have reappeared regularly," he said. "In fact, a man by the name of Bob Hedge fired at the ghost and the bullet holes are visible just outside of the windows. Hedge moved away, and in the following year seven families moved in and out, not being able to stay because they said the house was haunted."

According to Ernie Heegard, "Many scouts used to go up and look at the wall where they could see buckshot. And, the brother who was killed was often seen wandering around near the house."

There are other mysterious and potentially haunted spots throughout the reservation.

Lester spoke of an Indian burial ground at the foot of Buzzards Rock, a woman who was killed when a flash flood overturned her carriage as she attempted to ford the river, and other tales of intrigue at the Horseshoe.

Could it be that those spirits also stroll the camps?

Scouts in the 21st century have many diversions, many constructive activities that nurture their bodies and their character.

But on a dark night, around a campfire or in a quiet gathering, there could be nothing more invigorating than a good, old-fashioned ghost story to nurture that one vital part of a young person's very being—the imagination.

GHOSTS OF TOWN AND COUNTRY

This book may well have been subtitled "Book One," as it is certain that throughout the Brandywine Valley, as I have defined it herein, many more stories will emerge once those in this book have been published and read.

"How come you didn't write about..." and "Don't you know the story of..." will resonate from the lips and keyboards of people who have lived with ghosts in their homes or places well known locally as being haunted.

That's just the way it is. I like to chalk it up to "so many ghosts, so little time," or something like that. More than that, for publishing purposes, "so many ghosts, so few pages." To keep a regional ghost story book of this type within a popular price range, certain limitations are placed on the writer.

What follows are snippets of stories–what an old newspaper columnist friend called "smudged and tattered notes from a reporter's hip pocket"–that serve to let *you* know that *we* know these tales exist. Time restraints, memory lapses, or just plain sketchy information led to the stories being either incomplete or inconclusive.

Some are "they say" stories, such as the "Gates of Hell" and "Twin Bridges" accounts mentioned elsewhere. Some are pitifully paltry bits and pieces about spirit activity in an assortment of public and private places.

One very public place in Chester County is the official **Chester County Visitors Center** near the entrance of Longwood Gardens.

The center is set inside the former Longwood Meeting House, a ca. 1854 site of Quaker abolitionist rallies and a landmark on the area's extensive trail of "Underground Railroad" historic sites.

The former Longwood Meeting House

"The wind blows around," one volunteer at the center said, "and it sounds like there's a prayer meeting going on."

Speaking quietly and motioning toward an office storage area to the rear of the center's main gallery, the woman, who preferred to remain anonymous, added, "And...every once in a while you'll hear sounds as if someone is walking around out back."

"But, it's peaceful here. I have no fears here," she concluded.

In the center is a brochure that provides a self-guided walking tour of the Longwood Cemetery, directly across the street. In it are buried some of the area's leading early citizens, including the noted author and poet Bayard Taylor.

📖

They call their resident ghost "Dr. Todd" at the **Downingtown Library**.

Built in 1800 by Dr. William A. Todd, the building was also believed to have been instrumental in the "Underground Railroad," and was once a girls' school.

It became a library in 1912, and clerk Betty Boyd is convinced that it harbors a ghost or two.

"There's got to be somebody here," she confided. And, any time a card or a book or a paper is misplaced, or any time anything untoward happens, it's blamed on "Dr. Todd."

"I swear it's his ghost," Betty added.

📖

The management of a former estate that now serves as a country club did not want its ghost mentioned, so the exact location will not be revealed.

Suffice to say the historic clubhouse and grounds are supposedly inhabited by a phantom horseman and at least one ethereal individual who glides through the third floor corridors and rooms.

📖

And then there's the ghost of Ty Cobb.

Well, that's what the talk is at the **Parkesburg Arms Hotel**, owned since 1981 by Sid Kimes.

Built in 1907, the hotel has played host to many baseball greats (including Cobb) as they came into town to play games against the legendary local baseball team.

"They say you hear the crack of the bat and it's Ty Cobb," Kimes chuckled. Fully aware that it's all just a legend, he added, with a grin, "Yeah, he's still running the bases up there!"

The ghost of the Hall of Famer notwithstanding, Kimes was more serious when he admitted that if any place in the big hotel were haunted, it would be the basement. "There have been times down there when I'd hear something moving around. I'd listen, I'd watch, and I could never figure out what it was."

The **Stottsville Inn** is a fine country restaurant along Strasburg Road in Pomeroy. And, it wears its ghostly connection on its sleeve. Very well, then, on its *menu*.

It is one of the few places in the area where one may order an entrée named after the establishment's invisible (usually) and permanent (for sure) patron.

It is "Chicken Josephine." The chicken part is self-explanatory. The "Josephine" does not refer to a chef.

It refers to the woman whose forlorn ghost has been sensed on a staircase, in rest rooms, and certain

157

dining rooms of the ca. 1831 restaurant and guest-house.

Although the story may have been transfigured in the translation over the years, it is said that Josephine was a resident of the place many years ago. She was murdered there by her lover, a man named Horace.

This is where it gets interesting.

There is, beautifully framed on a wall near the front entrance of the inn, a suicide note left by none other than Horace. Although he is said to have killed her and then himself, the "note" tends to confuse.

An obvious "reproduction," the note reads, cryptically:

"I love, love, love, love you. You are the dream of my life. Come with me to the shoe store and I will make love to you. Love, Horace."

And, there is a postscript. It is a postscript in which Horace revealed his rather unorthodox form of suicide. He didn't shoot himself, poison himself, hang himself, or anything traditional. No, not our Horace:

"P.S. I can't live without you, so I will commit suicide in barn. I will bite a cow's leg and he will kick me in the head and kill me. For, without you, life is nothing."

Very well, Horace. Whatta way to go!

In the lovely main dining room of the Stottsville Inn is a cozy alcove they call "Josephine's Porch." It is from that vantage point, overlooking the side yard, where it is said the alive Josephine often sat and where the dead Josephine still lingers, waiting for a glimpse of the ghost of her beloved Horace.

📖

Somewhere in the vast "Great Valley" of eastern Chester County, described as between Conestoga and Pugh Roads and west of Valley Road, there lies an area once known popularly as **Hammer Hollow**.

Should you pinpoint the place, and the site of the old mill where an old man named Brown was killed, you may see or sense his ghost.

In the mid-1800s, old man Brown was manager of a local cigar factory and a minor evangelist. During one of his preaching sessions he sought to elevate himself from his "flock" by standing on a water wheel at a Hammer Hollow mill.

The water wheel moved, Brown fell, and the rest is haunted history.

📖

Much history has passed by and through the grounds of the **Ship Inn**, along Route 30 just east of Exton.

And, some of those who came to call may have come to stay there.

A tavern since 1796, the Ship once served drovers, wagon teamsters, soldiers, and stagecoach passengers. It now continues to serve its customers in a thoroughly modernized and chic atmosphere.

But, scratch away the snazzy décor and you will find remnants of the inn's rugged past. And, you might discover a ghost or two.

Personable proprietor Garrett Vlad (yes, Vlad, you Dracula fans) said there are plenty of reasons to believe the Ship is more than a little bit haunted.

You won't find any skeletons hidden in its walls, but those walls are themselves skeletons of the building's earlier configuration.

Although the Ship has retained its colonial elegance on the outside, its dining rooms and bar areas have been totally renovated.

Not so for the upper levels. "It gets creepy up there," Vlad admitted.

There's an overwhelming feeling some workers get, the feeling that someone is standing just out of their view, just over their shoulder.

The Ship Inn

"There's a lot that goes on here," Vlad said. "People talk about it all the time. I hear stories of people seeing a man sitting at a table, or standing in a hallway. As quick as he is seen, he disappears."

It is altogether fitting that the Ship may harbor a spirit or two. My experience through more than 20 years of investigating hundreds of haunted places tells me that a building renovated to the extent that the lower floors of the old inn have been may very likely send the energies fleeing to more familiar surroundings, such as those on the upper, virtually untouched floors.

What takes place there is mostly standard "ghost stuff." But, it's enough to send even the most stalwart server packing.

"Some employees won't even go up there," Vlad continued. "Heck, sometimes I'd rather not!"

📖

Stories about ghosts at the **Newlin Grist Mill** have been circulating for many years.

160

Former residents of the miller's house reported seeing a crying woman there, and respected mediums confirmed her presence.

As detailed in the book, *In Search of Ghosts*, by Elizabeth Hoffman, that spirit was sent from the miller's house to a more peaceful place.

That gentle exorcism aside, there are some who work or volunteer at the Glen Mills historical park who maintain to this day that the woman's ghost remains there, and may have been joined by others in the ca. 1739 miller's house.

The miller's house, Newlin Park.

📖

Officials at **Brandywine Battlefield State Park** have steadfastly denied the presence of any ghosts on their grounds.

Very well.

However, several authors, mediums, and paranormal investigators have detected very profound and high-level hauntings on and around the site of the bloodiest one-day battle of the Revolutionary War.

The fighting actually spread out across the Chester and Delaware county countryside, and it is believed by several researchers that spirits of many of the more than 1,000 casualties may linger in pockets of land where the battle raged and where modern housing and commercial developments now stand.

📖

No book on ghosts in Chester and Delaware counties would be complete without mention of the **Heilbron Mansion,** on Rose Tree Road in Middletown Township, Delaware County.

Built in 1837 and gutted by a disastrous blaze in the 1980s, the mansion has been rebuilt and stands as a private residence.

It was the setting of the book *Night Stalks the Mansion,* and was haunted by three spirits. The story centers on Margaret Edwards, who was raped and murdered there in 1864 by a handyman named Elisha Culbert.

Margaret's mother discovered her daughter's body and in a fit of grief hanged herself in an upstairs room.

An enraged mob of vigilantes tracked Culbert down and lynched him from a tree on the property.

The ghosts of all three have been known to haunt the mansion and its grounds.

📖

CLOSE ENCOUNTERS
OF THE GHOSTLY KIND

What follows are several accounts of unexplainable encounters with the spirit world as told by real people from Chester and Delaware counties.

Haunted graveyards, taverns, and mansions notwithstanding, it is from these sources, these average Johns and Janes, that the very crux of ghost stories emerge.

Note something as you read the following stories. Note that in more cases than not, the real names and actual addresses involved are not given. It is an awkward trade, anonymity for credibility, but you are asked to understand the reasoning and believe that each of the stories came from those Johns and Janes of the world who would prefer that their identities remain vague.

They may be your friends, neighbors, coworkers, or relatives. It is for that reason many of them do not wish to "come out" with their stories. Some fear ridicule. Some fear a loss of trust from clients and customers. Some fear their lives and homes becoming attractions for thrill seeking ghost hunters.

Whatever their reasons, their wishes are to be granted by me, and, hopefully, understood by you.

📖

The first story comes from not a nameless John or Jane, but from Amy DiPiano, an emergency medical technician from Montgomery County who resided in Chester County for many years. She had no problem with her real name being used, but I have chosen to disguise the precise locations of the incidents.

163

Amy was at her grandmother's house in East Coventry Township when she had the first of several brushes with the unknown.

"Just down the road from my grandmother's house," Amy said, "was a burial site for Revolutionary War soldiers. Strange lights have been seen in that cemetery at Elliswoods and Buckwalter Roads."

The monument at the Ellis Woods cemetery, a graveyard
said to be haunted by the spirits of Revolutionary War casualties.

With an obvious interest in the supernatural and in history, Amy told of her earliest recollection.

"I was very small, about four or five years old and I was sleeping over. It was around Easter and that may have contributed to an overactive imagination, but it is something that to this day I can still remember seeing.

"The house layout was an 'L' shape where from the bedrooms you could see right down the hall into the dining room and kitchen. I got up to use the bathroom and it was pretty dark, when I saw some kind of white misty shape move from the dining room and through the basement door.

"I assumed it was the Easter bunny," she chuckled, "and ran back into my grandmother's bed instead of my own. I never told my family of this until one day they were all sitting around the table talking about things past. That was when my mother recalled a time before I was born when, during a Thanksgiving dinner, that basement door started to rattle.

"This seemed to go all too well with the fact that none of us ever felt comfortable in the basement alone, almost like we were being watched. The feeling was especially strong in the two back rooms of the basement where my grandmother stored her deceased mother's and father's belongings."

Later in her life, Amy took up residence at two locations in Spring City.

"My first apartment was a three-story structure on Chestnut Street," she recalled. "That is where objects would repeatedly move on their own and where my old roommate reported seeing someone standing in the middle of the second bedroom when she would walk by.

"My second apartment was at the corner of Yost and Cedar Avenues. To get into the apartment you had to come up the staircase along the side of the building into the door and then up four more steps before you got in. Many times, at all hours, I could hear what sounded like someone running up the steps. The first few times I would go see who it was and find no one.

"I would hear scratches, thumps, and growls coming from the back bedroom. I hated to be there alone."

📖

The next story takes us to West Whiteland Township, Chester County, and to the rustic home of Adalee Flaherty, a teacher, adventurer, and outdoor enthusiast.

"I'm curious about everything," the ebullient woman said as we sat in the so-called Stone Room of her historic house.

That property has a name, but to reveal the name would be to compromise its location. Suffice to say it is all that remains from the storied past of a sprawling estate that is now consumed by an upscale residential development not far from the bustle of busy Route 100.

Adalee's Stone Room is festooned with symbols of her celebratory philosophy–Celtic and Native American art, a Circle of Life statuary, photographs of natural wonders such as the Devil's Tower, etc., etc.

"I'm very enthusiastic about life," she continued. "Since I was very young, I've always had special feelings. It was part of my growing up."

Weaned on tales told by her Irish relatives, Adalee holds history and folklore dear to her heart. An avid Civil War reenactor, she seems to be able to transplant herself into times and places far off in time and space.

Still, she is firmly rooted in reality–and certain *unrealities* that surround her in her comfortable home.

That home is the last vestige of a sprawling property that once included a manor house and outbuildings, including a carriage house. It is within the walls of that carriage house that she resides.

There are other reminders of the property's past, a bell once used to signal dinnertime, a swimming pool, stone walls and foundations, etc.

Amid the battles, skirmishes, and troop movements that criss-crossed that part of Chester County, anguished individuals doubtlessly inhabited her property.

And, perhaps it still is!

Adalee believes that beyond its Revolutionary War connections, the old "big house" was a popular spot for passers-by, and by folks who fled frenetic Philadelphia for the tranquility of the countryside.

"We kept as much intact as we could," she said, wearing the pride in her home on her sleeve.

Something she could not have expected to find, however, were the spirits of her haven.

Under a stone archway that leads from the newer part of the home into the Stone Room is a swirl of energy that manifests itself from time to time in several forms.

"We'll hear voices," she said, pointing toward the archway, "like a murmuring, over here. But there has been much more."

Indeed, the encounters go far beyond that archway and murmuring.

"There was one occasion when my fiancé's daughter and I were in an upstairs bedroom when she asked me if I thought there might be ghosts in the house.

"At that moment, at the precise moment she said the word 'ghost,' the light went off."

The two snapped into stares into each other's eyes. They could not believe what had happened.

As quickly and mysteriously as the light went out, it flashed back on.

Again, the women stared in disbelief.

Kiddingly, Adalee advised the girl that maybe she shouldn't say the word "ghost." Maybe just saying that word, she chided, stirred up the spirits.

"And when *I* said that word, the light went off again," she said.

The light flickered on again, and again they tempted whatever force might have been with them. Again, they said the word "ghost." Again, the light went off, and then on.

"At that," Adalee remembered, "she and I left the house. It was an overwhelming feeling."

That feeling pervades the home and extends far beyond electrical anomalies. Footsteps shuffle on staircases, groaning and sobbing sounds can be heard. Once, a full apparition of a male spirit was seen in that aforementioned stone archway. The energy has become so strong that it once chased an otherwise in-trepid housesitter away.

Adalee is a reader of Tarot cards, and in one par-ticular session, she sought answers from the entities that dwell in her domicile.

"The response was that they wanted to be re-membered," Adalee claimed. "They felt that things were changing around them too fast."

And who does she think the "they" might be?

There is some psychic evidence that the property is home to several ghosts, including a light-haired lit-tle boy who wanders near the site of an old well, and at least one other older individual who also tarries near that well.

It could be that the older ghost is a transient, per-haps a soldier on his way to or from a battle, with a stop in eternity.

The little boy, Adalee says, seems confused, searching for someone or something. It is his spirit that touches Adalee the most. She consciously tries to soothe his troubled soul.

In that old carriage house is yet another ghost, a more cantankerous spiral of energy that, according to one sensitive who visited the home, may be that of a woman who met an unpleasant fate there.

No matter what, Adalee, a woman in tune with the paranormal and in touch with the energies that wrap around her, feels quite safe in her home, and in the knowledge that the energies–the ghosts–there somehow need her calming understanding.

📖

The Route 724 corridor in northern Chester County is the setting for a bizarre incident and a ghost story as told by a man we shall know only as T.S.

"Shortly after we moved into Chester County from Montgomery County," he said, "my wife and I were driving past the Mt. Zion Cemetery on Route 724. She said she believed her father was buried somewhere in Mt. Zion. She was in her mid-forties at the time and her father had died when she was 13. She had not been to the gravesite since that time.

"A couple of weeks later I had to get some supplies in Pottstown. After purchasing my supplies, I started back toward Route 724. I hit a red light in Kenilworth when I reached the 724 intersection. I should have turned left to go home to Phoenixville, but something caused me to turn right.

"I thought that was strange, but it was as if something or someone was directing me to do what I was doing.

"I drove to the main gate of the Mt. Zion Cemetery and drove in. I drove a short distance and got out of the car.

"I walked to my left and immediately saw the tombstone of my wife's father's grave! The hair on the back of my neck stood up. I didn't tell my wife about the incident for a couple of weeks.

"I suggested we should go to the cemetery to put flowers on the grave. She said she wasn't sure exactly where he was buried.

GHOST STORIES OF CHESTER COUNTY and the BRANDYWINE VALLEY
"I told her I was, and she was amazed–to say the least–when I told her my little story."

But, T.S.'s brush with the unknown was to take a sharp turn toward the supernatural when he and his family moved into the Phoenixville home in which they still reside.

"We moved into the house in 1976," he said. "It seemed like a nice old house, built in 1903.

"We noticed strange sounds emanating from the third floor. My wife had her sewing machine up there in the back room and she would hear what sounded like footsteps on the hardwood floor in the front room. Our bedroom was directly below the front third floor room and we would sometimes hear a rocking chair on the floor directly above us. Our daughter also heard the sounds.

"There was no rocking chair up there! Strangely enough, we were not frightened by these sounds. We somehow sensed that whatever was there meant us no harm.

"The priest at our church asked my wife to make an altar cloth for the church, and she began sewing it on the third floor. She would occasionally hear the footsteps in the front room when she was up there in the back room. When the altar cloth was finished, the sounds stopped. We hung a crucifix up there and have heard nothing since 1978.

"I questioned an older neighbor about the history of our house and he told me that an old woman lived there until the early 1950s.

"She was found dead in her rocking chair in the front room on the third floor!"

It is to the farthest southern reaches of Chester County we travel for our next story.

In fact, we drove into this particular property in Pennsylvania, but drove away through Maryland.

170

Virginia Kelly's "Fair Tide Farm" is on a lane that leads north from State Line Road, a straight-line road that has the unique distinction of having its double-yellow line double as the Mason-Dixon Line.

Virginia's farm, actually not far from Nottingham, has had its share of legends and murky folklore attached to it.

Stories of nearby but long ago Ku Klux Klan activity–burning crosses and all–wallow in the dark lore of the area. What role did the property play in the Civil War? Was it a way station along the Underground Railroad?

Given that the big farmhouse was built around 1793 and given its location along the border that once divided a nation, Fair Tide may have many tales untold.

And, who knows what spirits dwell within the walls of that farmhouse and on the land that surrounds it?

Virginia Kelly would like to find out!

As she and her daughter, Caitlin, discussed their experiences, it was clear that within the pleasant rooms of their home are unsettled energies.

"Whatever is here," Virginia said, "it's not scary. It's not threatening. It doesn't do any harm. I think their pranksters."

The Kellys have lived in the house for 17 years, perhaps longer than anyone in the recent history of the property.

Winship Reed, who resides in another classic farmhouse just down the road and within sight of the Kellys, confirmed that he has seen a succession of owners move in and out of the place. He has lived in his farmhouse since 1976.

"And, those people talked about the same kind of things," Reed said. "The story line ran right straight through" each successive owner, he added.

That story line is a ghost story.

As Virginia noted, most of what happens in her home is innocuous. Items disappear and then reappear in the most unexpected places. Footsteps shuffle up the main staircase...and stop midway up.

Explaining that she has lived in older houses most of her life, Virginia said she knows the sounds such houses make. What she hears in her home–what she *feels* in her home–is not the norm.

She has seen what she can only describe as "orbs," floating globules of light that seem in accordance with "spirit lights" that have been seen by other people in other places.

In the former dairy barn that now houses the horses she boards, she and others have witnessed several phenomena, including the totally unexpected and seemingly impossible motion of a large, heavy, rusted door latch that, all of a sudden and without human aid, started to sway open and closed, open and closed, on its own.

Virginia said that when she tried to move that same latch in that same motion, she could not, with all her might, budge it.

Still, she and others watched. "That thing was like a pendulum," she marveled. "Just swinging back and forth on its own."

Virginia has heard her name called by an unseen voice. And, on one occasion, she might have had an unwitting and unlikely conversation with whatever or whomever haunts her house.

"I was here alone, right in front of the house, and I heard what I thought was my husband calling my name," she said, adding that what she heard was a pet name only her husband calls her.

"It was the middle of the day, and I asked him why he wasn't at work. He didn't answer me. Then,

I asked where he was. He said, 'I'm up here.' I said, 'Where?' He said 'Up here!'

"Because way the sunlight was at the time, when I looked into the house, everything was dark. And, of course, there was no one there. I was alone."

Or was she?

Winship Reed doesn't discount the possibility that a ghost or two might roam his neighbor's house. "I'm from Maine," he said. "We're full of legends and all that kind of stuff up there, so I don't rule that out."

Virginia Kelly said that her horse farm clients know about the spirit activity, and most find it interesting, amazing, or amusing.

A while ago, however, there was one chap who scoffed at the very idea of ghosts.

He was in the kitchen of the farmhouse while Virginia was in an adjacent powder room.

"I heard a loud crash," she said. "I came out of the bathroom and the guy was white as a sheet! The cabinet doors over the oven had flung open and a big earthenware platter had come out of the cabinet and crashed on the floor in front of him. It didn't break.

"And, he never questioned our ghost stories after that!"

Maria Watts is the manager of the Lionville landmark Vickers Tavern.

While that former home of Quaker abolitionist John Vickers has legendary connections with the "Underground Railroad" (with some supposed remnants thereof still visible), it appears to be free of any meaningful spirit activity.

But, it was at another Chester County site, an old eatery in Thorndale, where she was introduced to the unknown.

"The typical stuff would happen," she recalled. "Lights on and off, things like that.

"But then, there were the times that tray stands flew across the room and nobody was near them at all. It would freak people out.

The building, which was not operating as a restaurant at the time of this writing, had links to President James Buchanan and harbored many tales. Among them, Maria believed, were tales of the ghostly variety.

"My office was upstairs and there's a beautiful spiral staircase going upstairs. I would often hear footsteps up those stairs and go into the different rooms upstairs.

"It was pretty bizarre," she continued. "You could really feel it."

Maria also remembered–as do many natives of the Brandywine Valley–two oft-told tales of strange places where ghosts were said to wander and grotesque goings-on played out.

One is the "Twin Bridges." Literally, they are twin bridges along Valley Creek Road, along Valley Creek between Harmony Hill and Boot Roads.

Nothing more than an old legend remains there–the legend of a young girl who committed suicide by hanging herself from one of the bridges.

It is said that her ghost can still be seen–and heard–wandering around the "twin bridges" of East Bradford Township, Chester County.

Maria also told us, as others before her had, of the strange place known variously as the "Gates of Hell" or "Red Gates of Hell."

Lurid tales whispered down the alleys of generations regarding this mysterious place along Saw Mill Road south of Downingtown.

In reality, probably no one knows the truth about the "Gates of Hell." Ask any two individuals about it, and you are likely to get two wildly divergent stories.

If we were to not mention the "Twin Bridges," or the "Gates of Hell" in this book, however, we would be remiss. While they are probably more myth than mystery, they are representative of the types of settings typical in virtually any region of the country. They are the stuff of "urban legends" and adolescent adventures. But, they are also the stuff of local folklore.

While researching this book, we did speak to a Pennsylvania State Trooper at the Embreeville barracks. Coincidentally, he had just been in court with a large contingent of young people who had been arrested while trespassing on the property inside the "Gates of Hell."

The trooper, as well as all others in the police station, was all too familiar with the "gates." Said to be a portal to mystery, intrigue, and the occult for locals, they were once actual, ornate, iron gates.

Years of trespassing, tormenting, and taunting resulted in the mysterious disappearance of those gates. A fence replaced them, but that, too, fell victim of vandals.

In more recent times, only a chain was draped over the gravel lane that leads to the legendary local "haunted house."

📖

Quite possibly, the Chester County borough with the most hauntings per square mile is **Phoenixville**.

Over the years, accounts have circulated about a spirit in the attic of an old stone home at 501 Rossiter Ave., a phantom that prowled the house on Gay Street near Washington Avenue, where a medical facility now stands; and other buildings detailed in this book.

Along Route 724 adjacent to a popular seafood restaurant is the home of the renowned artist Mari Baum Landes.

We sat in her comfortable kitchen and talked of her life, her art, and her ghosts. Her wit and wisdom, tempered by her German/Irish ancestry, came to the fore throughout the conversation and belied her 80-plus years.

They have been good years, she assured us. And, a look around the family home easily revealed the fruits of her long labors.

Hundreds of her works of art splashed across the walls of a makeshift porch gallery and throughout other rooms and halls of the home. Landscapes, portraits, still lifes—no subject escaped her incredibly talented eye, mind, and brush.

Proud offspring displayed scrapbooks bulging with Mari's accomplishments throughout a most accomplished life.

The home, and Mari, comprise the epicenter of a strong family unit that spans several generations.

And that home and the land around it hold within them several legends and a ghost or two.

Even, it seems, some ghost dogs.

The main house was built in 1705 and, family tradition holds, was used as a field hospital during the Revolution. The grounds are tightly wedged between the restaurant and the roadway, and include an ancient bake oven, a small barn, and a carriage house, which has been rented as a separate residence. A larger barn once stood on the present site of the restaurant parking lot.

At any given time, any number of family members can be at the house. It is a warm, inviting place. It is also, by Mari Baum Landes' own assertion, a haunted place.

Undocumented stories claim there are Revolutionary War soldiers and Indians buried in unmarked graves on the property.

The spirits in the house have caused Mari and others in her family to wonder.

They wonder about the almost ever-present feeling that someone is following them as they walk through upstairs corridors. They wonder what causes lights to go off–and back on–without human aid.

They wonder about the validity of a friend's claim that she saw the ghostly images of Colonial-era men and women coast by her while she was in the living room. They appeared, and disappeared, in a flash.

Mari has had several experiences that have made her wonder more than anyone else has.

One she shall never forget happened after a long day in front of the canvas. Very tired, she trudged to the bedroom, where her husband was already in bed, sound asleep.

She lay there with barely enough energy left to pull up the covers. As if by magic, the sheet and blanket slowly moved up and unseen hands tucked her in. She glanced over to her husband, who was still sound asleep. She was too tired to be scared.

"That's the honest-to-God truth," Mari told us. "Now," she asked, "how could that happen?"

It was one of many secrets she has shared with only a few people.

On another occasion, Mari came down from the second floor into the rustic dining room only to find every chair upside-down or totally rearranged.

That phenomenon was also reported by the folks who lived in the house some 60 years before Mari moved in.

The most incredible encounter in the house took place on a second-floor landing, where a pack of ghostly dogs has been seen scurrying about. And, while the ghosts of the house–canine and all–are generally benign, there is something else altogether in and around the barn across the yard.

"You wouldn't be afraid of the ghosts in the house," Mari said. "But in that barn, there was something, well, more frightening there."

She refused to elaborate. No amount of coaxing would prompt her to say any more about whatever it was–or is–that kindled such negative thoughts about an otherwise picturesque old barn.

Unless she shares it with family members, it shall likely remain Mari's secret. She has earned the right to have a secret or two.

Be it about the phantom puppies, the disheveled dining room, or the mysterious barn, Mari's words painted vivid mental pictures with the same alacrity that her hands have created such marvelous art throughout a most remarkable life.

An elaborate door knocker at Hibernia mansion

HAUNTINGS AT HIBERNIA

Southeastern Pennsylvania is dotted with a predominance of the reminders of the area's once-thriving and vital iron-making industries.

The National Park Service has preserved one of those reminders at Hopewell Furnace National Historic Site. But not far from Hopewell is another lesser-known and less spectacular relic of the age of iron, Hibernia.

And, Hibernia is haunted.

179

The name is derived from the Roman name for what is now Ireland. Although little remains from the most productive years of the ironworks (in 1850 there were two forges, a rolling mill, grist mill, and two furnaces clustered in the midst of several workers' homes), Hibernia has come to represent an important time in the history of Chester County.

Records indicate the first forge to convert pig iron into bar iron was built there by Samuel Downing (of the Downingtown Downings) in the late 18th century.

In 1821, Downing sold the property to Charles Brooke. Brooke's family had extensive knowledge of ironmaking, was well connected, (Charles is said to have kept the struggling, young Lukens Steel Co. afloat financially), and under Brooke the Hibernia furnaces reached peak production.

Today, Hibernia Park, at 800 acres, is the largest county-operated park, and the gem of that park is Hibernia Mansion.

The stucco façade, peachy orange in color, appears out of place in a land of brick and field stone. You learn later that the stucco was placed over original stone. It is one of many curiosities about the building.

When production of iron fizzled at Hibernia in the late 1800s, Philadelphia real estate lawyer Col. Franklin Swayne bought the land and let the remains of the iron works fall to the ravages of time.

In Swayne's time, there was some farming, some ice making, and sheep raising. But to the colonel, Hibernia was foxhunting territory.

The land was gentrified into an elegant gentleman's estate, far from Swayne's rigorous legal life in the big city.

Swayne died in 1924 and the property was willed to a cousin. That cousin used the estate rarely, and found the cost to maintain it prohibitive. In the mid-

1950s, the old mansion was vacated. In 1963, Chester County purchased the remaining lands and mansion for $130,000.

It took county workers ten years to repair the extensive damages done to the mansion by vandals, time, and neglect. The result of their labors is a solidification of a home built in at least three phases, and a splendid representation of the property as it might have looked in its days under the ownership of the fox-chasing Swayne.

Fragments of the rambling mansion remain from the 1700s, and it is generally regarded that Charles Brooke erected the main body of the building in the early 1800s. But, other than the ballroom addition, or east wing, built in 1904, little is known of the exact construction history of the place.

As one wanders through the home, certain eccentricities unfold.

Quarter-round turrets connect and balance the uneven east and west wings with the central, three-story home. A wide portico is at the top of steps that lead to the broad, grassy meadow over which the mansion presides. From a vantage point deep into the meadow, the mansion seems deceptively symmetrical

Swayne anglicized Hibernia to his decidedly British tastes. The stucco façade was applied over the stone walls and a wide extension was added to the front of the home to give it a more English look.

Because of that front extension, some windowsills are four feet deep and some windows open to nowhere.

Even the most magnificent room of all, the grand ballroom, served little purpose. Swayne married a British actress who demanded a proper English lifestyle in the rugged backcountry of Pennsylvania. He accommodated his love and had the ballroom added for her personal partying pleasure.

It is said that Mrs. Swayne threw only one party there, and it was so extravagant and expensive that it was her last.

It was also the last straw in what was apparently a short-lived marriage. Shortly after the baptism of the ballroom, the couple divorced and the new wing became a hollow reminder of true love's folly.

Hibernia Mansion

When darkness sets in, Hibernia Mansion can be a foreboding place. But, don't tell that to Laura Bryson, who has lived there for more than five years.

She's quite content there, despite the fact that she shares her lovely abode with any number of ghosts.

Most of the energy seems to be centered in the servants' quarters, in the north wing of the mansion.

Sources at Hibernia say the last room at the top of the stairs is the chamber where the activity seems to be centered.

Laura's litany of the unknown includes several sights, sounds, and sensations that would have sent someone with less fortitude heading for the front door posthaste.

Put yourself in her place. You are walking through your home and you feel someone touch your shoulder. You wheel around...no one.

You are checking yourself in the mirror when in the reflection you spy a man standing not far behind you, dressed to the nines in a tuxedo. You turn, he is gone.

Or, you pass by a rocking chair and gaze in amazement as it begins to rock back and forth on its own. There is no breeze, no noticeable motion that could set it off. One time, you are astounded as you discover that the rocker swayed so violently that it tipped itself over.

Voices? Commonplace. They are mostly of a young woman or girl. She is sobbing.

Footsteps? Heard often. They are heavy, as if a large man in boots strolls down the hall and toward the bedroom.

Just when you believe you might be allowing the old mansion to get the better of your imagination, you notice that your dogs, your otherwise fearless dogs, will cower and refuse to enter certain rooms.

You invite a relative to spend a night amid the beauty of the old ironmaster's mansion. She is pleased with the invitation. Until, that is, she hears the voices, the sobbing, and the footsteps. She vows, through nervous tears, never to stay there, ever again.

Is it the colonel's ghost that paces and appears? Is it Mrs. Swayne's spirit that sobs and rocks?

These mysteries make Hibernia a quite special—and quite haunted—mansion.

📖

BEWARE THE MIRROR

When William Penn came to the New World, he set aside eight large chunks of his "wood" as his personal manors.

One was the more than 8,300-acre Springton Manor, near Glenmoore.

Thanks to the Chester County Parks and Recreation Department, and through the largesse of its last private owners, Penn's proprietary land is now open for all to see.

Just don't look in the mirror!

Springton Manor spreads over the rolling hills where housing developments are muscling in among the red-roof barns and chalet-style homes that are peppered throughout the landscape.

All that are left of Penn's original manor are about 300 acres.

The existing manor house that overlooks a demonstration farm and nature trails of the county park was the home of industrialist George Bartol, who lived there into the early 20th century and whose heir, Eleanor Bartol, deeded the property to the conservation group Forward Lands. That association in turn gave the farm to the county in 1980.

The manor house has been restored and its main hall, music room, "bride's room," kitchen, and meeting rooms are available for public functions such as dinners, receptions, and weddings.

A certain natural eeriness frames the manor house. Branches from a pair of giant Penn oaks, "King" and

"Queen," spread their craggy silhouettes over hulking boulders that rise in the lawn of the property.

It is the supernatural that is germane to this book, however, and there is a dash of it within the walls of the big house.

Mary Jane Swisher was the custodial manager of Springton Manor for more than 15 years. She'd arrive early, stay late, and get to know the house and all its idiosyncrasies as well as anyone could.

She did recall certain sounds and sensations that would occasionally draw her attention, but she reckoned they were just the sounds of an old house on a windy hill.

"If there are any ghosts there," she said, "they'd be friendly ghosts, I could have handled that!"

Ms. Swisher further believed that if any spirits inhabited the Springton Manor house, they would likely be those of Bartol family members. "And," she added, "they would like what we've done to the place."

There was, however, one story she recalled from her days at the manor.

"The only story I ever heard came from a young fellow who lived in the main house," she recalled. "He used to say to me as I was leaving after an event at nighttime, 'Don't look in that mirror–you're gonna see people looking back at you!'"

Ever skeptical, Mary Jane pooh-poohed the notion. She knew in her heart that she would not see anyone else in the giant, framed mirror on the second floor landing. She knew that.

"But," she laughed, "for the longest time I didn't look in that mirror!"

ABOUT THE AUTHOR

Charles J. Adams III was born in Reading, Pennsylvania, in 1947 and resides there today. In addition to his books, Adams also writes regular features on travel and local legends in the *Reading Eagle* newspaper and has written travel stories for several other magazines and publications.

Host of the morning show, "Charlie & Company" on WEEU/830AM in Reading, Charlie has also written more than 20 books on ghost stories, legends, folklore, maritime disasters and train wrecks in the mid-Atlantic states.

In constant demand as a speaker and master of ceremonies for parades, concerts, and special events, Adams has been a keynote speaker at the International Ghost Hunters Alliance conventions in Gettysburg, Pa., and has been interviewed on ghostly topics in England, Ireland, South Africa, and on several American radio and television stations.

He has also appeared on The History Channel's "Haunted America: New York" episode and has organized and escorted tours of haunted places in the United States, England, and Scotland.

He served as a consultant for The History Channel's "Haunted Philadelphia" production, which debuted in December, 2000 and also appeared in a segment for The Learning Channel on hauntings and ghosts, which aired in October, 2000.

Adams was a consultant for MTV on an episode of its reality show "Fear," which aired in March, 2001, and was engaged in a similar capacity for a Travel Channel program about haunted places in New York City.

His stories have been selected for inclusion in such books as "Classic American Ghost Stories" (August House Publishing) and "HexCraft" (Llewellyn Publications).

ACKNOWLEDGEMENTS

INDIVIDUALS, ORGANIZATIONS
Laura L. Robb, Debbi Kerr, Dorothy Stavrides, Art Prater, Aureio Merced, Ann Wyeth McCoy, Alyson Elliott, John Barton Rettew III, T.R. Thompson, Thomas M. Baldwin, W. Thomas Waters, Ian D. Currie, Chester County Parks and Recreation Dept., Chester County Historical Society, Historical Society of the Phoenixville Area, Chadds Ford Historical Society, Melanie J. Kuebel, Erie County Historical Society, Linda L. Riley, Valley Forge Convention & Visitors Bureau, Chester County Library (and branches), Pennsylvania Department of Conservation & Natural Resources, Brandywine Conference & Visitors Bureau, Chester County Conference & Visitors Bureau, Library of Congress, Reading Public Library

BOOKS
The Trackless Trail, Frances Cloud Taylor, 1976; *In Search of Ghosts: Haunted Places in the Delaware Valley*, Elizabeth P. Hoffman, 1992; *Around the Boundaries of Chester County*, Wilmer W. MacElree, Esq., 1934; *Night Stalks the Mansion*, Constance Westbie and Harold Cameron, 1978; *Welcome Inn*, Ed Okonowicz, Jr., 1995; *Nelson's Biographical Dictionary and Historical Reference Book of Erie County, Pa.*, S.B. Nelson, 1896; *Pennsylvania Profiles*, Patrick M. Reynolds; *Ghosts in the Valley*, Adi-Kent Thomas Jeffrey; *Stories of the Falls of French Creek*, W. Edmunds Claussen, 1974; *Great House*, John Baird, 1984; *The Battle-Axes*, Charles Coleman Sellers, 1930;

PERIODICALS, NEWSPAPERS, ETC.
Daily Local News, Philadelphia Inquirer, The Phoenix, Wilmington Morning News, County Lines, Township Voice, Reading Eagle-Times, Kutztown University Keystone, Honey Brook Herald, Chester County Living, The History Channel, Delaware County Daily Times, Pottstown Mercury,

...and countless others who crossed our paths during the research phase of this book. Sincere apologies for any omissions.

All photographs by the author.
Postcards from the collection of the author.

To Kevin, Jen, Emily, Yanek, and Tess.